LOVING AMELIA

A CRIMSON ROSE NOVEL BOOK 3

CATHRYN CHANDLER

Cover art: carrie@cheekycovers.com

Proofreading/Edit: Behest Indie Novelist Services

❀ Created with Vellum

BOOKS BY CATHRYN CHANDLER

The Circle of Friends Series:

Believing in Dreams (Maggie & Ian)

Believing in Love (Beth & John)

Believing in Promises (Abby & Cade)

Only One Dream (Lillian & Charles)

Only One Love (Rayne & Tremain)

Only One Promise (Shannon & Luke)

Only One Beginning (Dina & Cook)

Box Sets:

The Believing In Series

The Only One Series

The Crimson Rose Novels:

The Marshal's Promise (Jules & Dorrie)

The Rancher's Dream (Robbie & Brenna)

Loving Amelia (Ethan & Amelia)

Be the first to receive notification of new releases. Subscribe to the mailing list here:

http://eepurl.com/bLBOtX

PROLOGUE

August 1854
San Francisco, California

"Come along, boy. Yer draggin' yer feet fer no reason." The short woman was built like a solid block, and was wearing baggy pants held up by a piece of rope tied around her middle, along with a long-sleeved cotton shirt. Her clunky work boots made a hard thump against the wooden walkway with every step she took.

Cracker dug his heels in and held his ground, despite his tender age of twelve, he was still strong enough to bring the old woman dragging him along to a complete stop.

"Shue, I don't want to go into that house." He stared up at the two-story structure built on a side of town he'd never been in before.

He didn't know this place. He didn't know the people he'd seen go into the house, dressed in their fancy clothes.

He wanted to go back to his hidey hole near the gaming hall in the center of the city.

"Well, Miss Shannon would want you here, so Mister Luke says you're gonna be." Shue kept a firm grip on the back of the boy's shirt as she gave him a good shake. "Didn't Miss Shannon bring you food when you were hungry, and look out for you like she was kin?"

Brushing the mop of dark hair out of his eyes, Cracker reluctantly nodded. He liked Miss Shannon, and that was a fact. He'd never been so scared as when she'd become trapped on that roof a little while back, and all on account of trying to save him from a beating.

There was no doubt that he owed Miss Shannon. But it didn't mean he was going into that house with all those strange people.

His head snapped back and forth when Shue gave him another shake. "And didn't Miss Shannon and Mister Luke save your life?'

"Let go of me, you're hurting my neck." Cracker thrashed around but had no success in dislodging the old woman's hand from his shirt. She was the only lady miner Cracker had ever met, but for all her ornery ways, she might as well have been a man. And a mean one at that.

"I'll be hurtin' yer backside if'n you don't git yerself into that house," Shue threatened. "You don't go disrespectin' the hand that helps you, boy."

Cracker stopped struggling and hung his head. "I know it. But I don't belong in there."

Shue eased up on her grip and squinted as she looked into the young boy's face. "Of course you don't, Cracker. I don't either. People like us, we don't even have proper names. You, me, yer friend, Slab, none of us are good enough to be in that house. And we never will be. But that don't mean we turn our backs on the folks who show us kindness."

She pointed toward the big house with the bank of windows all along the front. "There're folks in there who've been good to both of us. We need to respect that."

Giving in to the guilt the old miner had managed to stir up in him, Cracker finally nodded. "I'll go in. But just long enough for Miss Shannon to see that I was there."

"That's good enough." Shue let go of his shirt and gave him a firm push toward the flower-lined walkway. "Let's git goin' then."

Despite walking as slowly as he could without risking another shaking from Shue, it was only a minute or two before Cracker found himself standing in a large room, with candles lit everywhere.

Once he'd suffered through a very public hug from Shannon, Cracker stood to the side, watching her dance with Mister Luke and planning his escape back into the night.

A flash of pink suddenly caught his eye, and he half-turned his body to get a better look.

A little girl stood off to the side, her eyes riveted on the dancing couple. Cracker blinked when the candlelight caught the deep, rich sable color of her hair, showing just a hint of red. He'd never seen anyone like her, and when she turned her head and smiled at him, he was caught in the spell of deep-turquoise eyes. The most beautiful eyes he'd ever seen.

When she turned her head to giggle at something her friend had whispered in her ear, Cracker frowned. He wanted her to look back at him. But like a dream, she suddenly vanished amid the shifting bodies of all the much taller people around her.

"That's Ammie."

Cracker swiveled around and came face-to-face with a blond-haired boy who looked to be just a few years younger than him. He glanced back to the spot where the girl had stood, and then at the boy who was still grinning at him.

"I'm Jules."

Suddenly all too aware that he didn't have a proper name, as Shue had just pointed out to him, Cracker settled for a nod.

"Are you hungry? There's food laid out in the dining room."

Since he was always hungry, Cracker smiled. "I'll follow you."

As Jules sped off , Cracker trailed after him, repeating a single word to himself.

"Ammie."

1

October 1872
San Francisco, California

"MAKE him keep his weight on his hind legs, boy. You're sittin' too stiff."

Tandy's gravelly voice still carried the twang from his native Tennessee as it rang out across the corral. The old foreman's words registered just enough that Ethan automatically softened his back while he gritted his teeth as the big stallion did a sudden, sharp jerk to the left. Tightening his grip on the saddle horn to keep from being thrown off, Ethan squeezed his legs against the outraged horse's sides and concentrated on following its movements.

"And talk to him."

Ethan would have rolled his eyes if he'd been able to. He was more concerned with keeping his head from snapping off every time the horse twisted around like it was trying to tie itself into a knot. He was in no mood to be sweet-talking to the ornery animal.

Even though it had only taken Ethan a moment to process what Tandy was saying, it was enough of a distraction that he missed the subtle shift Mudslide make to his front legs until it was too late. Half a second later, the stallion gave a quick, hard shove with his hindquarters, lifting its rear high into the air and violently ridding itself of the unfamiliar weight on its back.

With his arms flailing helplessly through empty air, Ethan landed hard, knocking the wind out of him as the stallion pranced off, snorting victoriously as he trotted to the opposite end of the corral. Fighting to suck in a full breath of air, Ethan didn't dare waste the energy to flinch when a hard boot nudged firmly against his side.

"Anything broke, son? Leg, arm, or rib, maybe?"

Cracking open one eye, Ethan looked up into the bearded face with the weathered skin and dark eyes staring down at him. Tandy was dressed in his usual signature brown, from his shirt to his boots. The only other color on him was the solid gray of his hair, which was the same hue as the granite boulders dotting the hillsides around the ranch.

"Nothing broken." Ethan's voice sounded thin since he was still working at getting regular breaths of air into his lungs.

Tandy looked skeptical. "You sure? Haven't seen you move anythin' yet."

Ethan closed his eyes. With a grimace, he obediently complied, lifting an arm and then one leg an inch or so off the ground before trying again to take a deep breath with mixed results. He did manage to draw in more air but ended up in a coughing fit.

"I'm fine," he snapped out when he could manage to get a word out. "I just need a minute."

"You need more'n a minute, boy. Seems that horse dumping you into the mud hasn't shaken the mood out of you."

Rolling onto his knees, Ethan painfully pushed himself up until he was sitting back on his heels, his hands resting on his thighs as he waited for his breathing to even out. "What are you talking about, Tandy? I haven't been home long enough to settle into a mood."

"Mean," the foreman snorted out. "Short-tempered and as touchy as a baby with a sour stomach."

"What do you know about babies?" Ethan scoffed.

Tandy fisted his hands on his hips and scowled at the younger man still sitting in the dirt. "What I know is that you should have waited for Luke. You might be the best tracker west of the Rockies, but the boss is a lot better'n you at dealing with a stubborn horse."

The old foreman had managed the ranch for over two decades until he'd retired to a small cabin a couple of miles from the main ranch house. With his easy gait, and a smile showing two rows of perfect teeth that belied his sixty-plus years, Tandy still showed up at the ranch most days. He always collected a mug of coffee from the main house before wandering through the barn and corrals to hand out a steady flow of advice.

Which Ethan was not appreciating at the moment.

Tall with broad shoulders, Ethan certainly looked the part of a rancher, but there was no denying his easy-going brother-in-law, Luke, was much better with the horses. Or at all the ranch work, for that matter. But then Ethan had spent most of his childhood wandering the streets in the rapidly growing city that was a day's ride away. He hadn't come to live on the ranch until he was fourteen.

But the eighteen years since then still hadn't turned him into an expert at breaking horses to a saddle. With a loud grunt, Ethan went back to concentrating on his breathing. "Luke's busy rounding up strays on that hill section in the north."

Mudslide's loud trumpet call had Ethan sending a glare to the far side of the corral. That horse needed to be taught just who was in charge. But when Ethan made a move to get up, he suddenly found himself flat on his back again, and this time with Tandy's boot planted squarely on his chest. Narrowing his eyes, Ethan kept a stony silence as he shifted his glare from the offending boot to the face of the older man holding him down.

"There's no use in pretendin' you've suddenly turned into a rock, boy."

Ethan let out an exasperated snort. "I'm not a boy, Tandy."

The old rancher nodded his head. "No. You aren't. But you've been gone for most of the last five years, takin' on every stock delivery we've had, and the further away you needed to go, the better. But the first thing you've always done when you got back is find a reason to go into town."

That was true enough. But this time when he'd come home, Ethan had stubbornly kept his feet planted firmly on the ranch. On the long ride back from Oregon, he'd decided he wasn't going into town again unless he had a damn good reason. Determined to stick with that, he'd made a point of repeating it to himself every morning when he got up, and whenever he found himself thinking about saddling up his newest mare. Which only happened ten times or so during the day.

"Now Luke might have to face the problem of havin' to replace cowhands because your sour mood will be drivin' them off. Which means I'm not lettin' you up until I have your word that you'll go into town and put your mind at ease by at least settin' eyes on that girl."

Ethan's jaw tightened. Tandy didn't know what he was talking about.

When Ethan's glare grew hotter with a clear warning in their deep-brown depths, Tandy only shrugged. "I may look old to you, Ethan, but I can still keep you on the ground for as long as it takes. Do you hear me, boy?"

After a full minute of a staring contest, Ethan finally relaxed and closed his eyes.

His bones ached from the rattling Mudslide had given him, and he was purely tired of lying in the dirt. Besides, he did have a thing or two he'd like to discuss with his childhood friend who still resided in town and was now a US Marshal. It was a good enough reason to make the ride into San Francisco.

And that was all he was going to do there. Talk to Jules and maybe enjoy a good whiskey and a game of cards at The Crimson Rose. Stopping at the marshal's house should be enough socializing to satisfy everyone in the family. He didn't need to look in on anyone else.

With that settled in his mind, Ethan opened one eye and stared up at the old foreman.

"I hear you."

Tandy reached out a gnarled hand and helped Ethan haul himself to his feet. "You might try gettin' to know somethin' about her life. Could be you find you got more'n common than you think."

Bent over at the waist with his hands resting on his

upper thighs, Ethan lifted his head enough to glare at the older man.

"I'm going in to talk to Jules. That's all I need to do, and then I'll be coming back to the ranch."

2

"I'll do what I can, Mrs. Kirkus, but I really don't think your husband has a... well, ladybird, as you put it." Amelia did her best to inject more sympathy than amusement into her smile. Good heavens! The couple had six children. When would Mr. Kirkus ever find the time to be with another woman? Or the energy?

That last thought forced Amelia to quickly raise a slender hand to cover her mouth. She simply could not stop the smile so she did her best to hide it. She certainly didn't want to offend a client, although her business had grown enough over the past three years that she could easily afford to upset one or two.

Ammie, as her friends and family called her, had started Inquiries so she could help support her small household, and not be entirely dependent on her Uncle Charles and Aunt Lillian. She knew they were more than happy to give her whatever she wanted or needed, but that didn't stop her determination to make her own way in the world.

And no matter how often her charismatic gambler uncle

had insisted the money he'd spent to raise her ever since she was six years old was from the inheritance left to her by her father, Ammie suspected those funds had been depleted for some time. If there had been any at all.

Especially since Eli Jamison had been murdered almost twenty years ago.

As she always did, Ammie deliberately turned her thoughts away from her father's murder. She still remembered her uncle waking her up that night. He'd sat on the side of the big bed her tiny form had almost been lost in and drawn her into his arms. He'd cradled her against his chest as he explained that her papa would never be coming home again.

The ache that had taken a foothold in her heart that night had never completely faded away, in part because whoever had killed her father had never been caught. And it wasn't the only thing that had happened that night when her entire life had changed. Because when her father had died, so had her mother, although not in a physical sense. But dead, nevertheless.

At least as far as Ammie was concerned.

Shortly after the murder of her husband, Christine Jamison had returned to her high society life in New York, but without the burden of a child. She'd abandoned her only daughter to be raised by her brother-in-law. The morning Christine had sailed away from San Francisco was the last time Ammie had seen, or even spoken about, her mother.

A blessing, Ammie repeated to herself. Christine Jamison's departure brought a whole host of wonderful aunts and uncles, if not by blood then by choice, into her life. An extended family that had grown over the years, and Ammie adored each and every one of them.

The sound of a sob brought her attention back to Mrs. Kirkus. Ammie kept the smile on her face while she searched for a gentle way to tell her obviously distraught client to give up her insistence on this latest investigation. This was the third time in six months that the thin, weepy woman with the pale complexion and huge brown eyes had sought out help from Inquiries over her suspicions about her husband's supposedly shabby conduct.

Suspicions that Ammie had always found groundless but hadn't yet been convincing enough to keep Mrs. Kirkus from coming up with new ones. Which she did with the same regularity as the tides flowing in and out of the bay.

"Are you sure you want to have your husband followed again?" Ammie kept her tone matter-of-fact as she raised the tea cup with its hand-painted, vividly pink flowers to her lips and took a small sip. "I doubt if he's changed his habit of sitting in the lobby of the Parker House Hotel and reading the paper."

Ammie sent her gaze to the ceiling when the mention of the hotel sent her client into another bout of weeping into her already soggy handkerchief.

"A hotel," the long-suffering woman got out between loud sobs. "My husband spends every evening at a hotel."

Reading a paper. Holding onto her patience, Ammie set her teacup down and folded her hands in her lap. Her dark-brown hair, the rich color of sable with a strong hint of auburn woven through it, gleamed in the late afternoon light streaming into the room from the large front windows spanning one entire wall of the parlor.

She pursed her lips with their natural rose tint into a straight line. It might be time for the blunt truth, rather than extending unending sympathy for an injustice that simply didn't exist. Maybe that would jolt the weeping woman into accepting that her husband wasn't a philanderer.

"Your husband spends every evening in a hotel lobby, Mrs. Kirkus. He arrives at precisely eight o'clock with his newspaper tucked under his arm, and goes directly to a small nook off to the side that is rarely occupied." Ammie held up a hand and counted off the various points from the same report she'd received from her associate at the hotel every single time she'd asked him to check up on the father of six.

"He orders a small brandy, reads his paper for an hour, and then goes directly home." Ammie lowered her hand. "I don't think we'll find anything has changed. He seems to enjoy the same routine." *And apparently finds the busy lobby of the Parker House less hectic than his own household.* Ammie prudently kept that thought to herself.

"But this time I'm sure there's more to it," Mrs. Kirkus insisted. When she started twisting her handkerchief in her hands and a set of fresh tears appeared in her eyes, the head of Inquiries gave in.

"All right." Rising to her feet in one graceful movement, Ammie offered the perpetually distraught woman a kind smile. "We will be happy to look into this matter for you." But she couldn't help the sigh when she added, "again."

"Thank you so much." Mrs. Kirkus also stood, and the tears vanished as she gave the striking brunette a puzzled glance. "You always say '*we* will look into the matter', but I've never met anyone except you. How many staff work at Inquiries?"

Ammie smiled as she thought of the steadily expanding network of people she referred to as "associates". Most of them had either been residents in years past at her Aunt

Lillian's Orphan Ranch, or were currently working in the gaming halls, hotel, and shops of the rapidly growing city that had once been fueled first by gold, and now from the silver mines in the mountains to the east. Not to mention the businesses and trade pouring in every day because of the new railroad service that spanned the entire continent.

"I'm not entirely sure." Ammie deliberately kept her response vague. She'd found that it was not only easier to keep the details about Inquiries simple, but the mystery also added to her enterprise's reputation.

"Mr. Dormand has never confided that to you?"

The question wasn't unusual. Ammie had learned from her Aunt Lillian, a very successful businesswoman in her own right, that most people, especially the men, were only willing to entrust their business to a man. Since she couldn't turn herself into one, Ammie had simply invented a never-seen owner, Mr. Dormand, to attract more clients. The fact that he remained mysterious and insisted that all messages be passed to him through his female "assistant", only attracted more clients.

"No. Mr. Dormand likes to keep his secrets." Ammie nodded solemnly. "As do most people. And I'm sure you'd agree that he's certainly entitled to."

Mrs. Kirkus' eyes took on a shine, as if she'd just become part of an exclusive club. "Of course, I understand." She lowered her voice to a whisper. "You can never be absolutely sure who to trust. It wouldn't surprise me if you discovered that Mr. Kirkus has been meeting with one of my very own confidantes. I'm sure they're quite fascinated by the stories I've told them about my husband." She gave Ammie an apologetic smile. "I wish I could share one or two of them with you, but I very much doubt that Mr. Kirkus could resist any overtures from one of the most beautiful women in the city."

Ammie politely smiled at the backhanded compliment, while her mind conjured up a picture of the unassuming Mr. Kirkus, with his narrow shoulders and thinning hair. She couldn't imagine the man doing anything that would even remotely attract one of Mrs. Kirkus' friends, no matter what stories they were being told about him. But the adoring shine in his wife's eyes simply reinforced Ammie's belief that love truly was blind.

"Thank you for not putting such a temptation in my path. Can I see you out?"

The matron picked up her small reticule and unceremoniously shoved her soggy handkerchief inside. "No, no. I can find my way, thank you." She scooted around the highly polished table separating the two divans that were placed near the large fireplace, and with one last nod accompanied by a watery smile, walked out of the parlor and into the front foyer.

Ammie remained standing until she heard the front door open and then close. Once Mrs. Kirkus had made her exit, the younger woman sank onto the divan and leaned her head back. She'd pen a quick note to Marcus, who'd been working in the public lounge at the Parker House for several decades. Ammie remembered her Uncle Charles mentioning once that the barman had been at the hotel even back when he'd been courting Aunt Lillian. Maybe she'd even ask the long-time hotel attendant about that very unusual courtship. It was sure to be more exciting than hearing about how long Mr. Kirkus had been sitting in the lobby.

Her amusement at the idea was interrupted by a voice rolling across the parlor.

"I thought that woman would never leave. Whatever did she want this time?"

Charlotte Jamison was the oldest of the Jamison siblings, and the only sister of her youngest brother, Charles. Tall, with the same sausage-sized curls that she'd favored for as long as Ammie could remember, Charlotte reached up and patted the gray swirls that were pulled away from her face by a wide pink ribbon.

Charlotte favored the color and used it every chance she got. Ammie wasn't even sure her aunt owned a garment that didn't at least have a splash of pink in it. Even the parlor was awash in the color, from the fabric covering the divans and chairs, to the wallpaper and the floral pattern woven into several large rugs covering most of the floor.

As eccentric as Charlotte was, Ammie adored the woman who'd left her comfortable family plantation back in Virginia many years ago to help raise her abandoned niece.

Ammie smiled as her aunt continued to sail into the room. "You know I never discuss my clients, Aunt Charlotte." At the older woman's disappointed look, Ammie relented just a little. "Although I can say that I haven't the slightest doubt that Mrs. Kirkus' fears will be put to rest, and I am crushed that she no longer considers me the most beautiful woman in the city."

"What nonsense." Charlotte's matter-of-fact tone had Ammie laughing. "Who does she think is more beautiful?"

Ammie shrugged. "I have no idea. But she usually makes a big point of saying I'm the most beautiful woman, and today she said I'm merely *one* of the most beautiful." Ammie let out a huge dramatic sigh. "Such a disappointment."

"Never known you to be vain, Amelia. I thought I taught

you better than that." The gravelly, decidedly male voice lacked any heat despite the words.

Jumping up from her seat on the divan, Ammie rushed across the room toward the tall gangly man with the long spider-like arms. The whole family simply called him Cook, since he had an extraordinary skill in the kitchen. He was also the silently acknowledged head of the large group who'd formed into a family by choice, and especially to Ammie and her Aunt Lillian.

The long-limbed man who'd once sailed most of the oceans in the world, had raised Lillian when she'd been orphaned at a young age, and then did the same with Ammie by helping Aunt Charlotte manage the household. Cook had lived with them for several years, filling both the role of house manager and protector, until he'd married Dina and moved himself and his new wife into a home of their own.

If Ammie had always secretly considered her Uncle Charles and Aunt Lillian as her mother and father, then Cook was most definitely her grandfather. Ammie gave the sailor-turned-cook a long hug before doing the same to the short, sturdily built woman standing beside him with a wide smile on her face.

"Aunt Dina, it's wonderful to see you both." Ammie stepped back and beamed at the older couple as Dina laughed.

"I saw you yesterday, dear, but I'm just as glad to see you today." Dina's eyes shone with amusement.

"I'm so fortunate Dina stopped by," Charlotte declared. "I'd still be in the kitchen listening to Helen's dire predictions if my good friend and her husband hadn't come along to rescue me."

"You love hearing Helen's predictions, no matter how

dire they may be," Dina admonished. "They're quite astonishing."

Their current housekeeper was known all through Charlotte's group of close friends as having "the sight". While her aunt and her friends enjoyed their regular sessions with Helen, Ammie and Cook had always done their best to avoid getting involved in the woman's "foretellings". In Ammie's opinion, which she was always careful to keep to herself, Helen's vision of future events tended to be far too gloomy.

As if she was aware that she was being discussed, the housekeeper appeared in the doorway carrying a large tea tray piled high with cups and saucers, along with two pots emitting steam from under their lids. Helen, who matched Aunt Charlotte in height and age, flashed her toothy grin at the group gathered just inside the doorway to the parlor.

"I expect all of you know what those chairs are for. Why don't you make use of them? I brought coffee as well as fresh tea for those who prefer it." Just as she always did, Helen ended her comment about "tea" with a loud sniff. Neither she, Charlotte, nor Cook ever touched the stuff, preferring a strong cup of coffee to the fragrant brew that Ammie and her Aunt Lillian always drank.

Once everyone had settled into a seat with the beverage of their choosing, Cook turned a stern eye on his former charge. "You have any new clients that I should be worried about?"

Not entirely sure what Cook had heard from the gossip mill that continually churned all over town, Ammie settled for a light shrug. "Mrs. Kirkus wants her newspaper-reading husband spied on for a night or two."

When Cook continued to stare at her, she averted her eyes and stalled for a bit of time by dropping a lump of sugar into her tea. "Harry Stanton has a bank customer who he needs a little research on."

Cook continued to stay silent as he studied her. He finally crossed his long arms over his chest and frowned. "Heard a few rumors about a merchant whose partner has disappeared. Along with a good amount of their money. That merchant hasn't found his way to you, has he?"

"Oh, I certainly hope not. The missing partner might very well be a thief, and those things are best left to Cade and Jules," Charlotte declared, referring to the two men in the family who were not only brothers, but US Marshals as well.

"Yes. It certainly should be handled by Cade or Jules." Ammie smiled at her aunt and then at Cook, who didn't look the least bit fooled by her innocent tone.

The merchant, Mr. Sanders, had indeed contacted her just the day before. Something she did not want to tell Cook since she was sure he'd raise a very vocal objection to this latest client of Inquiries. Worse yet, he might feel it necessary to tell her Uncle Charles, or any of the other overly protective males in the family.

Unfortunately, despite her quick agreement with Aunt Charlotte's declaration about letting the marshals handle the situation, Ammie didn't miss the look Cook sent her. It silently promised the discussion was far from over.

"I received a note from Lillian this morning."

Grateful for the distraction, Ammie's gaze turned back to her Aunt Charlotte, who lifted an eyebrow at her niece.

"Lillian expects you to attend the Lewis' party next Saturday evening. She wanted me to tell you that she will not accept any excuses from you."

It wasn't exactly a topic of conversation that Ammie would have preferred to discuss. The society events were not high on her list of favorite things, but more of a necessary evil since it was where most of her clients, or prospective ones, first contacted her.

Despite Charlotte's valiant efforts, Ammie didn't have many friends within the more elite social classes of the city. The petty jealousies, and what she'd always considered the boring activities of visits to dressmakers and afternoon gossip sessions, had never been appealing to her. Nor did she care for the participants in those activities since they only seemed concerned with snagging a suitable husband or exchanging vocal opinions on the latest scandals in the city.

Ammie had only made two exceptions to her avoid-friends-in-society rule— Christa, who was the youngest daughter of the reigning matron among San Francisco's elite, and her older brother Adam, a man of both wealth and charm, who offered little explanation on his personal life. But since both had started out as clients and then become friends, she didn't consider either of them as part of the rigid upper-class society she'd always done her best to avoid.

Rather than come up with one of her usual excuses about attending a party at one of the mansions dotting Nob Hill, Ammie nodded. "I'll be there, of course."

And she would be. Adam had sent word that morning that he had an urgent matter to discuss with her, and the Lewis' party would provide the perfect opportunity.

"Dina also told me that Ethan came into town last night and had dinner with Jules and his wife, Dorrie," Charlotte went on, seemingly oblivious to the sudden stiffening in Ammie's spine. "I do hope I'll have a chance to visit with him too. I haven't seen the boy in such an age, and I miss hearing about all his adventures."

"He does seem to enjoy wandering about the wilderness." Ammie couldn't keep the testiness out of her tone, and pretended she hadn't noticed the glance exchanged between Dina and Cook. Not wanting to dwell on the subject of Ethan Mayes and his frequent disappearances, she drew in a deep breath then managed a smile. "I'll send a note to Dorrie and have her send Ethan over. He'll come if she asks him to."

And I'll make sure I'm out calling on someone, Ammie thought. If Ethan Mayes couldn't be bothered to let her know he was in town, then she wouldn't be bothered to be home when he came to visit Aunt Charlotte. Ammie felt a tiny twinge of guilt at treating a childhood friend in such a petty way, but Ethan always did have a knack for bringing out that side in her.

"Of course, of course, that's an excellent idea." Dina nodded before turning a smile on her husband. "We'd best be going." She turned her gaze to Helen. "Thank you for all the wonderful refreshments." Her smile grew a bit. "You put an extra cup onto the tray, so I was hoping someone else might be dropping by."

"Soon," was all Helen said, which made Charlotte's mouth drop and Ammie's eyes roll upward.

"Fine." Cook's tone clearly conveyed the message that he was not going to sit and listen to any of Helen's babbles about the future. He got his long legs underneath him and stood, turning to help his wife up from the divan. He tucked her hand into the crook of his arm and sent Ammie a steady look. "I'll be by tomorrow to finish our talk."

Ammie's expression gave nothing away as her mouth curved up into a cheeky smile. "Wonderful."

Cook's lips twitched at the corners even as he shook his

head at her. With a last nod to Helen and Charlotte, the couple made their way toward the front door.

Putting aside the sticky problem of Cook's determination to discuss a client she had no intention of declining, Ammie settled in with her aunt and housekeeper for their afternoon ritual of a cozy chat, exchanging amusing tidbits about their day.

A good hour had passed by when they heard the sharp knock echoing across the front foyer. Charlotte quickly rose to her feet and crossed the room to peek around the curtain draped to the side of the window.

"I can't see our visitor, but it's a fine carriage." She glanced over her shoulder at her niece. "Are you expecting another client this afternoon?"

Ammie shook her head. "No, and I only take prearranged appointments."

A wide smile broke out on Charlotte's face. "Then it must be a gentleman caller. We haven't had many this week."

"Only four," Ammie complained under her breath before she turned in her chair and narrowed her eyes on Helen's back. The housekeeper was already making her way toward the parlor door. "Tell him I have a headache and am indisposed."

Helen looked over her shoulder and grinned at her. "Don't I always?"

As the older woman disappeared out the door, Charlotte's hands went to her hips. "You do indeed have Helen tell your callers that very same thing. I declare, all of society must think you do nothing but languish in your bed with a pile of headache powders."

"You'd think that would discourage them," Ammie

cheerfully agreed. "But these suitors are annoyingly persistent."

"And fortunate for you that they are," her Aunt shot back. "You are well past the age to be married, and your appeal won't last forever. It's time you considered one of these young gentlemen."

"I should think so. Being unmarried at twenty-five is very concerning."

A sudden wave of pure ice flooded Ammie's whole body and left her struggling to even breathe. Suddenly the years dropped away and she was back in that big bed, her arms wrapped around her uncle's neck as she tried so hard to understand what he was saying. Slowly rising from the divan, Ammie turned to face the open doorway into the parlor.

A woman with the features of a classic beauty, set off by black hair and a perfect ivory complexion, stood just inside the room. Her hands clasped a pair of white gloves as she smoothed out the skirt of a fashionable and flattering silk gown of midnight blue. And there was no mistaking the air of privilege surrounding her, as if it was an invisible cloak that was emphasized by the large diamond ring on the third finger of her left hand.

"Your housekeeper said to show myself in." Their visitor's nose wrinkled slightly as she glanced around the room before fixing her gaze on Ammie.

Clasping her hands in front of her to keep them from balling into fists, Ammie stared back at the woman with the deep-turquoise eyes that were an exact mirror of her own.

A sudden, light-headed rush reminded her that she was holding her breath. Ammie slowly took in air as she called on every ounce of her inner strength to put on a calm face. She finally tilted her head to one side in a perfect imitation of her Aunt Lillian, to acknowledge the stranger's presence. She ignored the continuing series of loud gasps and sputters coming from her Aunt Charlotte.

"I'm twenty-six, but then it's easy to lose track when you haven't seen someone in a decade or two." Ammie smiled politely when the woman's expression hardened in an obviously annoyed reaction to her very cool tone.

"Hello, Mother. What an unexpected surprise."

3

"It's nice to know you haven't forgotten me, Amelia." Ammie's long-absent parent took another step into the room before turning slightly to nod at Charlotte, who stood rooted next to the front window.

"And it's also good to see you again, Charlotte. I gather you had a hand in the room's decor? I recall that you favored the color pink."

"What are you doing here, Christine?" Charlotte's low and ragged voice was punctuated by her quickened breathing.

The dark-haired woman narrowed her eyes but kept a polite smile on her lips. "Not a very gracious greeting after so many years."

"What were you expecting after deserting your daughter and signing her away to Charles?" Charlotte retorted. "A welcome-home dinner party?"

Ammie frowned as her gaze shifted between the two women. Signed away? What did her aunt mean by that?

"I hardly expected a dinner party," her mother continued smoothly. "But a cup of tea would be nice."

"Tea?"

Charlotte stared at the tray Helen had brought into the parlor, her eyes going immediately to the extra cup and saucer. Following the direction of her gaze, Ammie remained silent for another long moment before dismissing Helen's mysterious tea cup. There were more immediate matters to deal with than the housekeeper's gloomy predictions.

"Why are you here?" Ammie lifted one eyebrow as she repeated Charlotte's question. Judging by their visitor's pursed lips, Ammie didn't think her mother approved of the question or the tone it was asked in, which was unfortunate for Christine. Ammie had no intention of offering any more of a welcome than that.

"Yes, well, perhaps it's best if we keep this first meeting as brief as possible." Without waiting for an invitation, Christine walked across the room and gracefully lowered herself onto a chair next to the divan. With a wave of her hand, she indicated that Ammie should also take a seat.

Still dealing with the inner turmoil her mother's unexpected appearance had caused, and resentful of the haughty command, Ammie stayed on her feet and defiantly took up a position in front of the fireplace. She kept an intense stare on Christine while her aunt crossed the room and stood beside her.

Charlotte put an arm around her niece's shoulders and glared at her former sister-in-law. "I have no intention of leaving Ammie alone with you."

Christine's generous mouth turned up at the corners. "There's no need since my business concerns both of you."

"What business?" Ammie demanded.

Her mother's gaze shifted back to her. She studied her daughter in silence before letting out a short sigh.

"It's about your father."

ETHAN PICKED up the telegram that Charles Jamison had slid across the desk. With his dark hair and eyes, along with a tall muscular build, Charles could have easily passed as an older version of Ethan. Something Lillian had commented on several times.

The younger man read through the short sentences on the paper, then looked up to find his honorary aunt smiling at him. She was standing behind Charles, her hands resting on his shoulders. Lillian's moonlight-platinum-blond hair and crystal-blue eyes were the perfect contrast to her husband's dark good looks. And no one would ever dispute that she'd been the reigning beauty during the city's gold-rush days.

As far as Ethan was concerned, she still was.

He soaked in the warmth of her gaze as he smiled back at her. Lillian had always had a way of making him feel loved, more like the mother he'd never known than the sisterly affection he felt around Shannon. Of course, he'd never spoken to Lillian about it. He would never be able to find right words.

"What do you think, Ethan?" Charles asked. "Do you know this Upland fellow that John mentioned in his telegram?"

Nodding, Ethan reread the last piece of the message. "He works for John's family. What does he mean when he says here at the bottom that 'I lost him'?" The younger man gave Charles a puzzled look. "John lost who? Has he spent all this time back East looking for someone?"

Charles' features instantly settled into the blank expression that Ethan easily recognized as the lifelong gambler's card-playing face. Usually whenever he was bluffing.

"It's a long story and has nothing to do with your instructions from John."

Certain he wouldn't get more of an answer than that, Ethan shrugged and set the telegram down. "Upland is one of the Davis Shipping Company's cargo handlers. John thinks he's sending crates of merchandise unrecorded to someone in San Francisco. He's had complaints of missing cargo from several customers. And it's looking like all the cargoes were sent out from New York where Upland works."

"So a thief," Lillian concluded. "And John thinks this Upland has a partner here?"

Ethan tapped a finger on the open telegram. "It would seem so. He gave me the name of the ship two of the crates are on. All I have to do is keep a watch on them after they arrive."

"And track the thief to wherever he's hiding the stolen items," Lillian said. "What we'd like to know is what you intend to do once you find this partner and his hiding hole?"

The dark-haired tracker exchanged a quick grin with Charles before giving his purely honorary aunt a properly serious look. "Why, I'll run and fetch Jules, or maybe the city sheriff, of course."

"Of course." Lillian's tone was as dry as the dust on the streets. "And I'll be happy to tell Shannon that you were hurt while dutifully fetching the law to help you."

"Thank you," Ethan said gravely, breaking into another grin when Lillian shook her head and glared at him. Giving her a wink, he turned his attention back to her husband. "When is John coming back?"

"Soon, I'd think." Charles plucked a slim cheroot from a

crystal jar on his desk and rolled it between his long fingers. "I believe he's concluded his business in New York."

"Now that he's lost whoever it was that he was looking for, that you won't tell me about?" Ethan didn't know why, but the missing piece of information was putting an itch between his shoulder blades. *If John went back East to track someone down, why didn't he take me with him?*

Charles reached up and covered the hand Lillian had placed back on his shoulder with one of his own. The small gesture wasn't lost on Ethan, and made that itch grow stronger.

"It's old business," Charles finally said. "And probably best left alone."

"Or maybe you don't need to go looking somewhere else for it." The voice ended on a loud intake of breath.

All three of the room's occupants turned and looked toward the doorway leading into the back hall of The Crimson Rose. Helen stood in the entrance, clasping the ends of a shawl wrapped tightly around her shoulders. Strands of gray hair floated out from the bun at the nape of her neck as she stared wildly into the room. Her chest was visibly heaving enough that Lillian immediately crossed the space between them and led her to the chair next to Ethan's.

"Sit." Lillian pressed a firm hand against Helen's shoulders until the older woman sank onto the edge of the seat. "I'll get you a glass of water."

"Whiskey would be better." Helen pointed a wobbly finger at the decanter on the gleaming mahogany table behind Charles. While Lillian poured her a short glass, Helen focused an unblinking stare on Charles.

"You don't need to go looking for that business," she repeated. "That business has come to you."

Frowning, the gambler leaned forward and planted his

forearms on the top of his desk. "What are you talking about, Helen?"

"There's a visitor at Ammie's house." Helen accepted the glass from Lillian's outstretched hand and raised it to her mouth.

Beside her, Ethan's back stiffened. *A visitor at Ammie's? What visitor would make Helen come running for Charles?* He frowned at the housekeeper as Ammie's uncle strode to the open door and shouted down the hall to have their horses saddled.

"Who's at Ammie's house?" Ethan demanded.

Helen turned her head and sent him a censoring glare. "Don't use that tone with me, Ethan Mayes, even if it is Ammie who I'm talking about." She sniffed at the younger man's menacing scowl. "You need to get to her right now. I told you trouble was coming. And now it's here."

Ethan stood to his full six feet and scowled at Helen. "What sort of trouble?"

"Calm down, Ethan," Lillian ordered. She came around the desk and knelt beside Helen's chair. Taking both of her old friend's hands in her own, Lillian gave them a light squeeze. "Who is at Ammie's house?"

"I've never seen her before, and didn't wait to get an introduction," Helen said. "But I knew the minute I opened the front door and laid eyes on her. She said her name was Mrs. Aldrin, but she was someone else before that, I'd stake my life on it." The housekeeper's head bobbed rapidly up and down. "And I've seen her shadow in my dreams but didn't know it was her until she showed up on our doorstep."

Helen stared into Lillian's eyes and then looked over at Charles. "She's the spitting image of our girl. She has to be Ammie's mother."

The room went as quiet as death. Ethan's gaze flew first to Lillian and then to her husband. In that instant he knew that for all her strange ways, Helen was speaking the truth. He could see it in the shock on Lillian's face and the leap of hot anger in Charles' eyes.

"Ammie's mother is alive?"

Ethan watched as Charles gave a brief nod and opened a drawer on the side of the desk. His eyes widened when the gambler drew out a small gun, stood up and dropped it into the pocket of the coat he retrieved from a standing rack next to the mahogany table.

Ethan blinked twice before looking over at Lillian. "But Ammie's never mentioned her. No one has. I always thought she was dead."

"Unfortunately not." Lillian sighed and rose to her feet, keeping one hand on Helen's shoulder. "Really, Charles? You aren't going to shoot the woman."

Her husband's lips turned up into a grim-looking smile. "Why not? Helen's right. Whatever reason brings her here only means trouble."

Lillian sighed again and walked over to stand in front of her husband. She raised a hand and laid it alongside his cheek. "Let's find out why she's here first."

Charles turned his head and laid a kiss into the palm of his wife's hand before gently taking it in his own and lowering it to hold against his chest. "Fine. And then I'll shoot her." He finally chuckled at Lillian's annoyed frown. "And not 'we', sweetheart. I don't want you going anywhere near that woman."

"I'm going. Ammie will need me now and I love her as much as you do."

"Me too," Ethan blurted out, picking up his hat and slapping it on his head to hide his embarrassment as three sets of astonished eyes turned in his direction. "I meant that I'm going too."

"We know what you meant, Ethan," Lillian said gently before gesturing to the door. "We need to be going." She glanced over at Helen. "You stay here and rest."

The tall, long-faced housekeeper jumped to her feet. "Not a chance, Lillian Smith Jamison. Ammie needs her family around her now, and that includes me."

Charles merely shrugged and grabbed Lillian's hand as he headed for the door with the tracker right on their heels.

ETHAN'S NERVES drew tighter as the minutes passed. Thank god Charles hadn't been willing to wait until the buggy was hitched up for Helen, but had ordered his stableman to bring the housekeeper along when the carriage was ready. Even with that concession, Ethan still arrived at Charlotte and Ammie's house first.

He slid off the back of his tall mare with the dark-brown coat and strode up the porch steps with Charles and Lillian only a few paces behind him. Not bothering to knock, Ethan shoved open the front door and kept right on going, turning right and striding through the door leading into the parlor.

His gaze immediately went to Ammie, who was standing in front of the fireplace. He did a quick assessment of her face, frowning at how pale she looked. Her Aunt Charlotte was seated in a chair looking just as stunned as her niece.

Ethan didn't even bother to glance at the woman sitting across from Charlotte as his long legs quickly carried him across the room. Stopping in front of Ammie, he deliberately used his broad shoulders and back to block out her view of the rest of the room as he studied her upturned face.

"Are you all right?"

"I'm fine, Ethan."

His gaze narrowed when she drew in a ragged breath. Her shoulders were stiff, and Ethan could plainly see the slight tremble of her lips.

"I don't believe you've met our guest."

When Ammie gestured behind him, Ethan threw a glance over his shoulder. His mouth dropped open when he finally got a good look at the unexpected visitor.

She was a perfect older, darker-haired version of Ammie. No wonder Helen was instantly sure this was Ammie's mother. When the woman raised one eyebrow at him, Ethan's jaw tightened.

No matter how much the two women resembled each other, or what claim the woman thought she had on her daughter, he wasn't going to stand quietly by and allow this stranger to hurt Ammie. Slowly turning to face her, Ethan tried to keep Ammie behind him, but wasn't surprised when she quickly stepped around until she was standing by his side.

"No. I haven't met her," Ethan finally said, then nodded at the two people standing behind the seated woman. "But your aunt and uncle have."

Satisfied with the audible gasp that statement drew from Ammie's visitor, Ethan didn't move a muscle when her eyes shot wide open and she twisted in her chair. Her back went noticeably stiff as soon as she was caught in Charles' hard stare.

"Christine. I thought we had a bargain."

His former sister-in-law raised her chin a notch. "Which I have kept for many years, Charles. But circumstances have demanded that it be set aside. At least temporarily."

She straightened out in her chair so her back was once

again to Charles and Lillian. "Amelia was to be my first stop, and then I intended to pay a call on you, so it's fortunate you're here now. It won't be necessary for me to repeat myself."

Lillian stepped forward, bringing a reluctant Charles with her. She walked slowly to one of the divans and sat, staring at Charles until he ran a frustrated hand through his hair and finally lowered himself to sit beside her. Turning toward the woman carefully watching them, Lillian smiled.

"Hello, Christine."

Ethan felt a small jolt of surprise when the haughty Christine retreated back against her chair and gave Lillian a cautious look. A shadow of a smile crossed Ethan's lips. It seemed the haughty woman was more leery of Lillian than she was of her former brother-in-law.

Christine shifted her gaze to a point beyond the calm, platinum-haired beauty sitting across from her. "It's pleasant to see you again. I know from your correspondence that it's Lillian Jamison now, isn't it?"

The former madam tilted her head to the side. "Yes, it is."

"Do you have any children?"

"Three, as a matter of fact."

"Who you will not be meeting," Charles said abruptly.

In the ensuing silence, Ethan decided to follow Lillian's example. Wrapping a large hand around Ammie's lower arm, he tugged her over to the nearest chair. A firm push on one of her shoulders forced her to sit. Ignoring the glare she shot at him, Ethan braced his legs apart, crossed his arms over his chest, and stood guard as he waited to hear what this Christine had to say.

Charles took one of Lillian's hands in his and leaned

back against the divan. "Well, Christine? Tell us what's brought you here, and then kindly leave this house."

When Christine glanced over at Ammie, Ethan waited until she'd shifted her gaze to him before slowly nodding his agreement. Since it was more than obvious that none of the family wanted to see Christine Jamison, the woman could state her business and then go back to wherever she came from.

"Very well." Christine took a moment to smooth her skirt across her knees before looking directly at Charles. "If Mr. Hawkes is not already here in San Francisco, he will be shortly."

"Oh no." Charlotte had been sitting quietly, but now all the color drained from her face as one hand flew to her throat.

Beside Ethan, Ammie turned in her chair to peek around him at her pink-clad aunt. "Who is Mr. Hawkes?"

Charlotte's mouth opened but not a sound came out as her gaze shot over to her younger brother. Charles' expression had turned to stone, his stare fixed on Christine.

Lillian exhaled a loud breath before taking in another one as she turned an unhappy look toward her niece. Ethan instinctively took a smaller step closer to the chair Ammie was sitting in and braced himself.

"Simeon Hawkes." Lillian frowned as she briefly hesitated before adding in a soft voice, "the man who murdered your father."

4

"I THOUGHT YOU'D LEFT."

"Nope."

When Ethan didn't say anything else, Ammie's mouth thinned out. "Why not? I was very clear that the visit was over, so you aren't obligated to stay."

Ethan raised an eyebrow. "Your visitor left. I'm family."

"So are Uncle Charles and Aunt Lillian, and I'm sure it hasn't escaped your notice that they've gone home."

He dropped his arms to his side and frowned at her. "What's bothering you?"

Ammie pressed her lips even tighter together to keep from snapping out at him. Standing there in his dusty boots, with his dark good looks and steady gaze, he looked so very... she searched for a word but her mind went blank. He was simply Ethan. Tall, strong, quietly intense. She barely remembered a time when he hadn't been a constant in her life.

At least that had been true when they'd been growing up.

But he'd been mostly absent the last five years, and right

now she was too overwhelmed by everything that had happened that morning to have to deal with Ethan too. And wasn't this just like the man? When she'd desperately wanted him around, he was nowhere to be found. And now that all she longed for was a bit of solitude, he wouldn't go away.

Ammie put her hands on her hips and frowned at him. "Why do you think anything is bothering me? Everything is fine. Now will you please leave?"

"I didn't know your mother was still alive," he finally said quietly. "You've never mentioned her."

Feeling suddenly drained, Ammie walked over and laid a hand on the back of one of the divans. "There was no reason to. And truthfully, I rarely thought of her."

"But you did think of her at times?"

Ammie's shoulders slumped. "Yes."

"You never told me a word about her."

Sucking in a quick breath, Ammie's eyes narrowed. She didn't care for the slightly accusatory note she'd heard in his voice. It's not as if they were still in the habit of exchanging confidences, so he had no reason to be put out with her. And who's fault was that? *She* wasn't the one constantly running off.

"There wasn't anything to tell, Ethan. I haven't seen her since I was six years old. And you were standing right there when Aunt Lillian admitted she's been writing to Christine for years, and I've never known a thing about it." She straightened away from the divan. "Now. If that's all?"

"What do you know about your father's murder?"

Not nearly as much as I'm going to, Ammie thought, but she had no intention of sharing that with Ethan Mayes. He'd probably make sure she was locked inside her room.

All the men in the family had a tendency to be absurdly

overprotective as far as Ammie was concerned. Her honorary cousin and best friend, Dorrie, had once called it their habit of "circling the wagons". And Ammie also seemed to remember Dorrie mentioning something about being packed away in cotton balls. If Ethan had any thoughts along those lines, she was going to have to set him straight.

She wasn't about to be shoved aside when it came to her father's murder.

"I don't know much about it. And until tonight, I had no idea Uncle Charles and John had almost been killed themselves."

Ethan frowned, his gaze remaining steady on her face. "From someone Charles called a 'ghost killer'. What did he mean by that?"

"I have no idea," Ammie admitted, then added hopefully, "maybe you should go and ask him yourself?"

Ethan rubbed a large hand against the side of his cheek. "I need to get back to the ranch, but I can't leave you here alone."

Of course he had to go back to the ranch. Ammie looked away and rapidly blinked against the unwanted moisture in her eyes. "I'm not alone, Ethan. Helen and Aunt Charlotte are here, and what makes the difference if I'm alone or not?"

His arms were back to being crossed over his broad chest. "I'm not leaving you alone when there's a threat nearby."

"What threat? Surely you aren't talking about this Mr. Hawkes?" Genuinely surprised, Ammie's tears instantly dried up as she stared in astonishment at the scowling man.

Ethan's jaw went a little tighter. "Who else have we been talking about ever since I got here?"

Ammie gaped at him. "Why is he a threat to me? I was

little more than a baby when my father was murdered, and I doubt if papa ever brought the man around and introduced him to the family. It seems to me that this Mr. Hawkes would have more of a grievance with Uncle Charles or Aunt Lilian. Either of them could recognize him, I'm sure." She tilted her head to the side and stared at him. "Why don't you go guard *them*?"

"You don't know who he's a threat to," Ethan insisted.

"Neither do you," Ammie shot back. "And I'm sure he isn't the least bit interested in me."

"You have an objection to extra protection being in the house?"

Ethan was using his "I'm-trying-to-be-reasonable-with-you" tone of voice that Ammie had always disliked. Especially since she'd only heard him use it with her.

Mimicking his stance, she crossed her own arms and glared back at him. "I'll ask Cook if I need to."

Ethan shrugged. "All right. I'll go with you and we'll both ask him."

"If there's a need after I read the letter that's coming, I'll certainly let you know." Despite her gritted teeth, Ammie managed to keep her tone polite.

He only snorted at that. "A letter from someone who's offered you nothing before this, despite the vast resources he's supposed to have? Why is he being so generous in keeping you informed now?"

The tears were back, and this time she completely turned away from Ethan to keep them hidden from his watchful eyes. The last thing she wanted was his pity for being abandoned by a large piece of her family. "No. He hasn't ever offered me anything. But then neither has Christine, who said herself that she signed away her rights to even visit me."

"Ammie, these people don't care about you, and..."

"I know that." Ammie interrupted him, wrapping her arms around her waist as she glared at him. Why would he think she wasn't painfully aware of that? A mother who hadn't wanted her? A grandfather she hadn't even known about?

It was one thing to have been orphaned the way their childhood friends Robbie and Dorrie had been. Even Ethan had lost both his parents to death. But it was quite different not to be wanted at all.

Much to her mortification, Ammie's chin began to tremble, so she quickly turned away from Ethan. Lord! She really did not want to cry in front of him. All she wanted right now was to be left alone. If Ethan was only worried that there wasn't a male about the place, she could remedy that quickly enough and he could be on his way.

"I'll arrange for a guard to watch the house as soon as I can. But right now I need to see to Aunt Charlotte, and you said you needed to get back to the ranch." She gave a quick glance and a nod over her shoulder before picking up her skirt with one hand. "Have a safe trip."

Ethan might not visit very often anymore, but she was sure he could find his own way to the front door. Not willing to stay one more minute, Ammie hurried out of the parlor. Turning toward the stairs, she lifted her skirt higher and vaulted up them two at a time, reaching the upper landing just as she heard the hard ring of boot steps crossing the entryway. She pressed herself against the wall in the hallway and held her breath, closing her eyes when the solid oak door leading into the house opened and then shut with a final thump.

Limp and defeated, Ammie dragged herself down the long corridor to her bedchamber at the end. She stood in the center, feeling more than a little lost and alone. What she needed was a good cry, but first there were a few notes she had to send out.

Heading for her small writing desk that was snuggled between two large windows against the far wall, Ammie sighed and positioned a blank piece of paper in front of her. Picking up a writing pen, she bit her lower lip as she waited for the trembling in her hand to subside.

After several minutes, she decided she could dip her pen into the bottle of ink she always kept available without making a mess of it. Ammie carefully set it on the paper and began to fashion her request for a meeting.

With that note finished, she quickly penned a second one to Dorrie. She needed to talk to someone, and who better than her best friend? And because they *were* best friends, Ammie felt no guilt in telling Dorrie to leave her husband, Jules, at home. She was not in any mood to put up with Jules, who would feel obligated to defend Ethan and his constant running off for parts unknown.

5

ETHAN LOOKED OVER THE ROLLING LANDSCAPE BEFORE turning his mount toward a tight cluster of trees next to a small pond. Always cautious when he was out in the open, he slowly guided Brat around the compact body of water, his gaze moving over the ground, looking for any new tracks since the light rain from the night before. Seeing nothing that raised an alarm, Ethan dismounted and walked his horse to the edge of the tree line before he turned and began to unbuckle the saddle.

He'd spent most of the last two days riding, and still had another four hours in front of him. He might not be the best ranch hand in these parts, but he was the best tracker. He knew the value of taking care of his horse, so he was going to let Brat rest for a while before pushing on.

When the chestnut swiveled her head around to watch what Ethan was doing, the tracker grinned at the animal. "Have I ever told you how much I appreciate you being so easy to understand?"

When his horse only blinked, Ethan nodded his head. "That's what I mean. When you want your saddle off, you stand still. When you want to eat, you go find some grass. You do what's expected, and that makes you easy to be around."

Ethan released the strap and lifted the saddle from Brat's back. "I wish people would act the same way." Especially a particular female who he was positive was planning on doing something he was sure would put a constant worry in his gut.

Ethan carried the saddle over to a small ring of rocks a former traveler had left for anyone coming after him, along with a pile of branches and twigs. Dropping his burden onto the ground, Ethan knelt down and started to build a fire. He was looking forward to the strong taste of coffee. It was always good to be outside and alone.

At least he thought he was alone.

A shimmer of movement along the bottom of a hill in the distance had Ethan stopping and squinting against the sun. Leaning over, he reached to the back side of his saddle to retrieve the spyglass he always carried with him. Lifting it to his eye, Ethan aimed it at the far hill, slowly quartering across the landscape until he came across a tall man sitting easily in the saddle of a horse with a dark coat.

A quick glimpse had him lowering the spyglass and carefully strapping it back into place. With a wide grin, Ethan finished building the fire as Brat meandered toward a patch of tall grass, dropping her head to take a nibble here and there along the way.

He figured he had about thirty minutes before he got company.

With that in mind, Ethan efficiently went through the chore of fetching a small pot of water and setting it next to the flames to heat. By the time the rider reached the pond, Ethan was leaning against his saddle, his long legs sprawled out in front of him and a mug of coffee cradled between his hands.

He lifted his tin cup by way of a greeting as the man with the piercing blue eyes and a badge pinned on his chest dismounted. "Out chasing bad men? Or are you running from married life?"

Jules McKenzie rolled his eyes before setting about removing his saddle and sending his dark stallion eagerly toward the spot where Brat was peacefully grazing.

Once he'd dropped the saddle on the opposite side of the fire, the marshal walked over and latched onto the mug Ethan was holding out to him.

"Thanks." He took a deep swallow, making an appreciative sound in the back of his throat. "Thought I'd have to ride longer and harder before I found you."

Ethan's eyebrows drew together. "You came looking for me? Is there trouble somewhere?"

Jules removed his broad-brimmed hat and set it on top of the saddle horn. "In my house if I didn't catch you." Jules' mouth turned up as he did a swift look around. "Although you're riding in the wrong direction if you're heading out. You usually hightail it to the north of the ranch, not south."

Ethan only grunted at the amusement in his friend's voice. The marshal knew exactly where his friend was headed. The tracker considered Jules more like a brother than an honorary cousin in their extended family. And like any brother, Jules did try to get him riled up at times. Which at the moment wouldn't be a hard thing to do.

"You rode all this way just to be sure I wasn't heading out again?" Ethan lifted a shoulder in a careless shrug. "The marshaling business must be pretty slow right now." He raised an eyebrow when Jules snorted. "What made you think I was heading out?"

"My wife told me you were," Jules said.

Ethan blinked. Dorrie? Now why would Dorrie think such a thing? "Where did she get that idea?"

"From Ammie."

"Ammie knows I wouldn't do that," Ethan grumbled. He narrowed his eyes when Jules' grin grew wider. "What's so funny?"

"Where *are* you headed? If you're delivering more stock to those ranchers up in the Oregon territory, you're not only headed the wrong way..." Jules paused and gave an exaggerated look around. "You also forgot the stock."

"You damn well know that I'm going into town."

Jules raised an eyebrow. "Oh? Then I wasted a ride. How long are you planning on staying?"

Crossing his arms over his chest, Ethan settled his back more firmly against his saddle. "Why? Are there limits to how long a man can stay in San Francisco?"

Jules shook his head, but his grin stayed in place. "Haven't heard of any, unless you've broken the law." When Ethan remained silent, the marshal chuckled. "You haven't broken any laws, have you?"

Not bothering to answer such a ridiculous question, Ethan leaned forward and grabbed the handle of the pot sitting by the side of the fire. He poured a fresh stream of coffee into his mug then held the pot out in Jules' direction in a silent question.

The marshal shook his head as he continued to study Ethan. The two men had been friends since Ethan was twelve and Jules was ten. After all those years, Ethan knew what that look meant. Jules had something on his mind.

"You aren't planning on breaking any laws are you, Ethan?"

Didn't take him long to get it out. Ethan set his mug aside and rested his elbow on top of a raised, bent knee. "That's a strange thing to ask, Jules."

"I know it." Jules blew out a long breath. "But we're walking new ground here from what I could get out of Dorrie. Which wasn't much." He paused and stared into the fire for a moment before lifting his gaze back to the man sitting on the other side of it. "I'd appreciate hearing from you what happened at Charlotte's house yesterday. All Dorrie told me was that she'd promised Ammie not to tell me anything, and that I had to come and get you and bring you back to town."

Now it was Ethan's turn to grin. "You took off for a full day's ride with no explanation of why? Just because your wife asked you to?"

"A wife who's going to be giving birth to our first child in a few months," Jules reminded him. "I've learned to keep her happy first and ask questions later."

"So, you figured you'd ride out and ask *me* the questions instead of dealing with your wife?"

"Thought it would be easier than trying to pry it out of Dorrie." Jules rubbed a hand across his chin. "Now. What happened at Charlotte's?"

"Ammie's mother showed up." When Jules didn't say anything to that, Ethan figured that Dorrie must have told him that much. "Christine came to give Ammie and Charles a warning that the man who murdered Ammie's father was on his way to San Francisco."

"What?" Jules' mouth dropped open. "Dorrie said Ammie was in danger and that's why you needed to be here and not taking off for Oregon again. She didn't say a word about a killer headed our way. She made it sound like Charles and Lillian needed extra protection and Ammie would be fine with just you."

Gratified that his friend was showing signs of the same anger and frustration that he'd felt ever since he'd run smack into Ammie's stubbornness, Ethan suddenly frowned. "What did she mean by 'just me'?"

"As opposed to the army of guards Dorrie and Ammie want me to hire to keep an eye on Charles and Lillian." Jules' dry tone said plainly enough what he thought of that idea. "Because of course Charles wouldn't lift a finger to protect Aunt Lillian." The marshal shook his head. "Like I said, there's no reasoning or arguing with a woman in my wife's current condition."

"Sounds like Ammie has convinced your wife that this ghost killer isn't any threat to her or the other women in her house," Ethan snorted. "She tried to convince me of the same thing."

"Ghost killer?"

Ethan nodded. "That's what Charles called him.

"What else did he have to say?"

"Not much." Ethan scowled. It was high on his list to pay a visit to The Crimson Rose and corner Charles to get the whole story out of him. Although that would certainly be easier said than done.

None of the uncles could be intimidated into doing anything unless they had a mind to. And Charles Jamison might be the worst of the lot.

"He only mentioned this ghost of his had almost killed John and him, and that this killer had worked with someone named Hawkes."

Jules gave a long, low whistle. "I wouldn't have bet there was anyone who could harm Charles or John, much less both of them."

"Which is why you and Cade need to keep a close eye on him and Lillian."

"If he'll let us," Jules said. "I suspect he'll be hiring a passel of guards himself." He grinned. "And what will *you* be doing?"

"What Dorrie wants me to do. I'll be watching Ammie."

"Is that a fact?" Jules grin had returned. "Last I heard, Ammie was under the impression that you were riding out. Which is why I had to come chasing after you."

"Not my fault she thought that way and then told your wife the same thing."

Jules' brow furrowed as he stared across the fire at his friend. "So you didn't tell Ammie you were going to the ranch?"

"I did."

"Did you tell her when you'd be back?" At Ethan's silence, Jules began to chuckle. "Well, that explains why I was sent to fetch you." He raised his eyes to the clouds above them. "Just how are you planning on telling one Amelia Jamison that you intend to watch her every move until this ghost killer is caught?"

Ethan shrugged. "Shouldn't be a problem since I'll be staying at the house."

The marshal's grin stretched wider across his face. "Have you told Ammie about this plan of yours?"

Well aware that she'd make several loud objections to him bunking down in her house, Ethan had already hit on a solution. "I only need Aunt Charlotte's permission. Robbie's stayed there, so have other family members. I don't think Charlotte will mind."

"Robbie only stayed there to annoy you," Jules pointed out. "And him staying in Ammie's house is a lot different than you staying there, and you know it."

Ethan didn't know anything of the sort. Robbie had grown up with Jules and Ethan. As boys, the three of them had been thick as thieves whenever they got together. Ethan also considered Robbie a brother, if not by blood, then by choice.

"We're both part of the family so I'm not seeing the difference."

Jules snorted out his disbelief. "Then what was your reason for telling that particular member of the family he couldn't stay at Ammie's again, or else?"

Trust the marshal not to forget something like that. Besides, he hadn't actually threatened Robbie. Exactly.

Uncomfortable, Ethan settled for a noncommittal shrug. "Robbie's not fit company most times. He likes poking his nose where it doesn't belong." Ethan dismissed the subject and concentrated on his plans to keep Ammie safe. "I need to talk to Charles and get a description of Hawkes, and anything else he can tell me about this ghost killer."

"I'll be going with you for that little talk with Charles," Jules stated. "But what are you going to do about Ammie? You can't believe she's going to stay in her house and knit while her father's killer is running loose?"

A sudden image of Ammie sitting quietly in an all-pink chair in the very pink parlor knitting a sock had Ethan stifling a laugh. No. He couldn't see her doing that in a million years. But she was going to have to find something to keep herself busy, because he wasn't going to let her out of the house until he had eliminated this potential threat. Or, she could go somewhere safer than her house in town.

His brow furrowed in thought. Her being far away from town was not a bad idea at all. "She won't have to stay inside long. I'm going to bring her out to the ranch."

Jules gaped at him. "How do you intend to do that? Hogtie her?"

"If I have to." Ethan's voice was firm. Ammie would be

safer out at the ranch. Then he'd go back into town and track down this Hawkes and make sure he never bothered Ammie, or anyone else in the family, again.

The marshal laughed. "And you really believe she'll go along with it?"

Ethan looked up at the sun to gauge the time, then leaned back against the saddle. "She'll come around once she figures out she doesn't have any choice in the matter."

Rolling his eyes, Jules shook his head at his friend. "Is that a fact?"

6

Ammie moved slowly along the boarded walk, its planks wet with the heavy moisture hanging in the air. The fog was rolling in from the bay and would soon shroud the entire city in a blanket of gray. Ammie reached into the deep pocket of the long, slightly tattered coat that fell to her knees, and cradled a watch in her hand. Drawing it out just enough for her to get a peek at the time, she quickly dropped it back into its hiding place and frowned. An hour past midnight. She hoped she hadn't missed her quarry.

Quickening her step, Ammie made sure to keep her head down. Her bulky scarf was wrapped securely around her neck and covered her chin and mouth. She was deep inside the area of the city known as the Barbary Coast, and the last thing Ammie needed was trouble.

Men slid past her on the walkway, intent on avoiding the perpetual mud of the streets. Most kept their hands in their pockets and their gazes constantly moving as they either looked for their next victim or tried not to be one.

In her shabby coat and britches, Ammie easily passed as one of the many urchins who lived on the streets and came out after sunset to forage for food and anything of value they could find. Which did not make her a desirable target for either the thieves roaming the area, or the ladies of the night plying their trade in the middle of the sea of men swarming along the walkways.

And on every block was at least one gaming hall, and often two that faced each other from opposite sides of a narrow street. Noise poured out of the open doors of the rowdy establishments Ammie passed by. She ignored the sounds and smells as she headed for one particular establishment. The one her newest client had mentioned. Well, her newest client if she didn't count Mrs. Kirkus' latest request.

Turning a corner, Ammie slowed her steps. In the middle of the block of shabby buildings, most with boards missing from their sides, was a gaming hall. Its bright-red door boasted large gaudy roses painted in gold down its length. A crowd of men stood outside, lounging against the outer walls, looking over the customers who stepped through the portal and disappeared into the cloud of cigar smoke and the low roar of voices that crashed out into the street.

The owner of The Golden Rose had done his best to imitate the much more elegant hall just a few minutes' walk from the central square of the city. But this clientele definitely came from a different part of the population than those who her uncle and aunt catered to at The Crimson Rose.

Not wanting to draw any unnecessary attention to herself, Ammie crossed the street, putting some effort into freeing each step from the mud that sucked at the bottom of her sturdy boots. Finding a spot hidden in the shadows with a good view of the bustling scene in front of the shabby gaming hall, Ammie leaned against the rotting wall at her back and slouched over. She stuffed her hands into her coat pockets and kept her chin down as she settled in to wait.

Thirty minutes later, she was stifling a yawn when she spotted two familiar figures as they passed by the light pouring out of The Golden Rose's doorway. Mouse and Wang Wei. They were part of the network of associates she had built in the city, and they usually worked with the man she'd come looking for.

Keeping her eyes on them as they moved out of the light and into the shadows, she shook her head when they both stopped at the far corner of the building, right next to the small alleyway that ran along the side of The Golden Rose. Crossing her arms, Ammie watched as the two young men took up a position on either side of the gap between the buildings and turned away from each other, acting all the world as if they had no idea who the other one was.

Rolling her eyes, Ammie settled back into her own casual stance. She knew who Mouse and Wang Wei were waiting for, and it was fortunate for her two associates that their target was less fit than they were, as well as a great deal more naïve.

A scant five minutes later, Ammie easily spotted him. The young man, with his perfectly cut trousers and coat and a high gloss on his obviously expensive boots, stood out like a lit torch in a cave.

"He might as well be shouting 'please rob me'," Ammie muttered under her breath as she watched his eager progress toward The Golden Rose.

In another moment he'd passed the alleyway, not even giving a glance to the two people standing on either side of its opening. Ammie didn't show a flicker of surprise when a long arm suddenly shot out of the darkness and the young man disappeared into the black hole before he could utter a squeak of protest.

Mouse and Wang Wei waited for several long moments before they both made a quick glance around and then disappeared after the young man. Half a minute later, they re-emerged, once again taking a careful look around before moving aside.

A huge man with hands the size of dinner plates, stepped out onto the wooden walkway, carrying something long and bulky over his shoulder. Ammie might have even believed it was a sack of grain if she hadn't seen the pair of hands hanging out from underneath a large square of rough cloth. They were flopping against the big man's back.

Clearly her associates had completed their assignment of corralling her latest client's son and stopping him from losing his entire allowance at the gaming tables. But Ammie wasn't at all sure that the stiff and proper Nathan Milton was going to appreciate his only son and heir being rendered unconscious and then carted about as if he were a dead body.

But at least she'd found who she'd come looking for. Once they'd had a little talk, she could be off for home and her very comfortable bed.

Sure that the odd threesome making their way to the distant corner of the street had a conveyance of some sort close by, Ammie straightened away from the building and broke into a fast walk, silently following them. When they disappeared around the corner, she had to change to a quick trot so she wouldn't lose them. By the time she spotted the threesome and their burden again, they'd already reached the back of a wagon that was hitched up to a single horse.

Using the big man's size to hide from the other two helping him maneuver young Milton into the wagon, she winced at the hard thud of her client's son being dumped onto the hard bed. A second later their human baggage let out a faint moan. The three cohorts were gleefully congratulating each other when Ammie reached out and gave a firm poke to the big man's wide shoulder.

"Excuse me. I seem to be lost."

When all three whirled around and stared at her with wide eyes, she put her hands on her hips and tilted her head to one side. "I'm looking for friends of mine who were supposed to be following a young gentleman and keeping him out of trouble."

Mouse and Wang Wei quickly ducked their heads while their older and much bigger companion gave Ammie a wide smile from beneath a bushy beard. He jerked a beefy thumb back toward the wagon. "He's not gittin' into no trouble now."

Ammie leaned to the side to look around William Milton's abductors. "I can see that. I can also see that he's out cold, Slab."

The tall, solidly built man who stood a good foot over Ammie's slender form, shrugged. "But he ain't in any trouble. And from what I saw, that's the only way the young fool was goin' to stay that way."

There wasn't much more she could do other than shake her head. Especially since she was sure that Slab was probably right. From what the father had told her, his son's gambling had gotten out of control.

"He was being followed when he left The Silver Dollar," Mouse spoke up. Ammie couldn't help but turn a smile on the slightly built young man who was a few years older than her, and had spent some time on her Aunt Lillian's ranch for orphans. He'd rarely spoken back then and didn't talk much more now. Which made him the perfect companion for

Wang Wei, who could easily manage to keep up a flow of chatter for hours if he wanted to.

As if he'd read her mind, the young Chinaman gave her a friendly smile. She could almost see the sparkle in his dark eyes despite the black night and the increasingly dense fog all around them.

"Mouse is right, Miss Amelia. There were some very bad men following our friend in the wagon, and they meant him harm."

Slab's crack of laughter echoed off the sides of the building and rolled down the street. "I don't think he'd consider us his friends, Wang Wei."

The younger man's smile grew wider. "Perhaps not. But someday he'll thank us for saving him from a painful beating." He held out his hands that he'd been keeping behind his back. "And you can see that these are returned to him. It's a nice watch he has. It's gold on the top with initials carved inside. Most likely a gift from his father. I remember when my grandfather gifted me with..."

"Just give what you got to Miss Amelia and try to keep quiet. This ain't no place for socializin'." Slab, who'd gained his nickname at a young age when his miner father had called him a "big slab of meat", gestured toward Mouse. "Then you take this feller and put him somewhere his own kind will find him."

"You'll do no such thing." Ammie had to choke back a laugh even as she firmly shook her head. "Take him over to Nob Hill and leave him on the porch of the fifth house on the left. It's made of brick and has an iron gate across the front garden."

She looked down at the stack of paper money, the watch, and three ten-dollar gold pieces that Wang Wei had placed in her hands. She stuffed the paper money and the watch into her pocket and held out the gold pieces. "Each of you take one. It's a bonus for keeping William Milton alive." As the gold swiftly disappeared from her hand, Ammie tilted her head and raised an eyebrow at Mouse. "And it's also part bribe. Be sure you get him home in one piece. Don't let me hear that he was found somewhere else."

"We'll get him home, Miss Ammie. Won't we, Mouse?" Wang Wei slapped a hand against his friend's shoulder.

Mouse didn't say a word, but nodded his agreement and started out for the front of the wagon. Wang Wei sprang after him as Ammie raised a hand in farewell. She waited until the sounds of the turning wagon wheels faded away before she turned her attention back to Slab.

"I hope you didn't hit him too hard. His father is a well-paying client after all."

Slab grinned. "His pa won't have no complaints. That young whelp took one look at me and fainted dead away. His head might hurt a bit where it hit the ground, but that weren't my doin'."

Ammie laughed. "I'll be sure to point that out to his father."

"What are you doin' out here, Miss Amelia? I would have been by yer house in the mornin'." Slab crossed his arms over his chest. "This ain't a good place fer you to be wanderin' about."

"I've been wandering about it for a few years now, Slab." She held up a quick hand when Slab opened his mouth. She wasn't here to argue with him about her safety. She had an entirely different topic on her mind. "I need to ask you something. It's about my father."

"*Your* father?" Slab's heavy eyebrows shot up. He looked away, studying a distant point for a long while before he turned his dark-eyed gaze back to her. "All right." He jerked his head to the side. "Let's walk closer to the square. It's too hard to talk and keep an eye out fer troublemakers."

As the two of them made their way out of the Barbary Coast, Slab kept up a continual scan of the doors, open alleyways, and streets around them. Lost in her own thoughts, Ammie walked along in silence, following her most trusted associate as he led them toward Portsmouth square, located in the center of the city. When they reached the busy hub, he stopped at a low wall made of stone, set away from the streaming crowds around the square.

"This is a good spot." He sat and patted a flat part of the wall next to him. "You can rest here while we talk, and then I'll walk with you to be sure you git home safe."

Ammie took the offered seat and looked around. Slab was right. Surrounded by trees with an easy view of the square so you could see without being seen, it was indeed a good spot.

"What do you want to know about your pa, Miss Amelia? I wasn't quite full growed, and was helpin' me own pa at his mine when yers was killed."

Ammie turned her body slightly to face him. "So you knew that he was murdered?"

Slab pursed his lips, but he didn't look away when he nodded. "I heard. Don't remember exactly when. I've heard more, but it wasn't about yer pa. And I don't know how much of it's true. Stories have a way of growin' as years pass."

Turning her gaze to the ground, Ammie considered what she already knew. Eli Jamison had been a fairly recent arrival to the city, and she was certain her Uncle Charles and Aunt Lillian had been much better known than her father. Which left only one tale that would have been told and retold over time. *The ghost killer. He's heard about the ghost killer.*

Taking a deep breath, she raised her eyes to look him squarely in the face. "I need to know what you've heard, Slab."

The big man frowned. "Why? It won't do you no good to think on it now. It won't change nothin', and like I said. I don't even know if any of it's true."

"He might be back." When Slab gave her a startled glance, Ammie nodded. "The man who's called the ghost killer might be back in San Francisco, and I'll need your help to find him."

SLAB WAS in the middle of a story he'd been told about the ghost killer who'd come within a hairsbreadth of making Charles Jamison one of his victims when he suddenly went silent. He reached out and wrapped a wide hand around Ammie's upper arm.

Taken completely by surprise, she swallowed a gasp and quickly followed the direction of his gaze. Her stare landed on a tall figure with wide shoulders and dark hair showing beneath the broad brim of his hat. He looked like any of a dozen cowhands still milling about at this late hour, but she'd have known that easy gait of his anywhere.

Ethan. And from the slow and careful way he was moving around the edges of the square, she knew he was looking for something. Or someone. And unless Dorrie had taken to sneaking out of the house right from under her husband's nose, Ammie had a good idea just who that "someone" was. She quietly scooted off the wall and faded deeper into the shadows as Slab went completely still.

"I'm too big for yer tracker not to notice once I move, Miss Amelia."

"He's not *my* tracker," Ammie whispered back, not even daring to blink. She was sure if she did, Ethan Mayes would disappear and sneak right up behind her.

"He's yer family," Slab responded. "He's lookin' fer somethin' and my guess is that's you. Maybe you oughta jist go over and let him know where you are? He'll find you anyway. Ethan Mayes always did find what he looked fer."

"Maybe so, Slab. But he has no business looking for me."

"Judgin' by the way he's actin', I'd say he don't agree with you." Slab shrugged. "You can try sneakin' back home, but I don't think you'd get there first."

Ammie pursed her lips. She struggled between being annoyed at seeing Ethan, and happy for the same reason. What was he doing here? She was sure he'd be halfway to the Oregon territory by now.

Irritated that she could never sort out her feelings whenever he was, or even wasn't, around, Ammie decided to be annoyed. Which meant she had no intention of facing some kind of inquisition about what she was up to. Especially not one from him. But Slab was right. Getting past Ethan would not be easy.

She was still considering the problem when Ethan stopped. He leaned against a post and slowly moved his head. Ammie knew he was quartering the area, and if she was going to get away, it had to be now.

"Slab. You'll have to distract him."

The big man's head whipped around. "Me? He'll take out that shooter of his and kill me."

"No, he won't," Ammie snorted. She was absolutely certain Ethan would never do anything like that. "Just go over and talk to him until I can get away."

Slab looked toward Ethan and then back at Ammie. "Is that all?"

"Yes. Just make sure he doesn't follow me. I only need a moment or two and I'll be safely on my way." She smiled. "I'd consider it a great favor."

The big man raised a hand and idly scratched behind his ear. Ammie waited quietly, her eyes still fixed on Ethan while Slab thought it over.

"All right. I'll make sure he don't follow you." Even though he nodded, Slab didn't sound too happy at the idea.

"Walk in that direction." Ammie pointed toward a far corner of the square. "Once he sees you, I'll be on my way."

"This ain't goin' to work," Slab muttered, but he got to his feet and stepped out onto the walkway as Ammie faded further back into the shadows.

She watched Ethan closely and knew the exact moment he spotted Slab. Ammie held her breath and stayed completely still when his narrow-eyed gaze swept to the area behind the big man before returning to following Slab's progress. Once the tracker moved to intercept Slab on the far side of the square, Ammie only waited long enough until his back was turned before she moved. She quickly looked up the street and gauged the distance until she'd be out of Ethan's sight.

She'd only taken her gaze off him for a moment, but it was enough.

"Ammie!"

She froze as her name rang out and then blinked when it was immediately followed by a shout and then a large splash. When she looked over her shoulder, her mouth dropped open. Slab was backing away from a wide water trough where Ethan was flailing about in the water. When the tracker took his hat off and threw it at the large man, Ammie started to laugh.

"Slab. You big jackass!"

The sound of Ethan's voice, laced with frustrated anger, finally jolted Ammie into moving her feet. Turning on her heels, she raced off. The square was a pleasant half-hour walk from her home, so Ammie figured without the hindrance of skirts and petticoats, she could make it to her front door in half that time.

When she finally reached the wide porch, she was gasping for air and there was a hard stitch in her side. Ammie managed to get her key into the door and then step into the entryway before sinking to her knees. She'd never run that far that fast and was certain she'd never be doing it again. She could barely drag enough air into her chest. But it was worth the agony of trying to breathe normally again. Now all she had to do was get up and lock the door, and everything would be fine.

Ammie started to struggle to her feet when suddenly an unyielding band of hardened muscle wound itself around her shoulders. Before she could summon the strength to even scream, another arm slid under her legs and scooped her off the ground.

7

"You make one sound and I'll drop you right on your backside." Ethan's voice was harsher than he'd meant it to be, but he was wrestling with the sudden and painful leap of heat in his blood when she'd flung her arms around his neck. Ignoring the pounding of his heart, he carried the breathless Ammie into the parlor and carefully laid her down on the divan. When she began to struggle to sit up, he simply put a large hand on top of her head and gently pushed her back down.

"You lie still until you stop gulping air in so fast you might keel over and hurt yourself."

He wasn't even a little surprised when she glared up at him.

"What do you care if I do?"

Ethan shrugged and ignored the squishing noise from his boots as he crossed his arms and shifted his weight from one foot to the other. "I don't want to have to fetch Doctor Abby to patch you up."

Ammie sniffed at that and took several deep breaths as

she wiggled her way to a sitting position. She looked down at her raggedy coat and made a face. "You got me all wet."

"Whose fault is that?" Ethan snorted. "You're the one who had Slab push me into the watering trough." He narrowed his eyes when it was clear she was fighting not to smile. "And you'd better not laugh about it, Amelia Jamison. Or there'll be hell to pay."

"Oh really?" Now Ammie's mouth did tweak upward at the corners. "Do tell what you intend to do about it?"

He raised an eyebrow at her. "Lock you in your room, comes to mind."

Ammie rolled her eyes and then looked past him and smiled. "Good evening, Aunt Charlotte. Look who's come to call on us again?"

"For goodness' sakes, what is going on? I could hear you two all the way from my bedchamber." Charlotte's gray hair flopped down from beneath her frilly nightcap, and she clutched a long bedrobe at her neck. She blinked several times before smiling. "Hello, Ethan. It's nice of you to come calling, but it is rather late, dear." Her head turned as Helen came shuffling into the room.

The housekeeper's feet were bare, and her night rail trailed along the floor. Ethan didn't budge when Ammie scrambled off the divan and took a long step away from him as Helen glared at them both.

"What are you doing here so late, boy?"

Ammie put her hands on her hips and gave him a smug smile. "I was about to ask him the very same thing?"

Ethan frowned at her. If she thought he was going to do the gentlemanly thing and take the blame for her sneaking around the city at night, she was going to be sorely disappointed.

"Chasing after you to make sure you got home in one piece."

"Did that require you to take a dunk in the bay?" Helen pointed at the puddle around his boots. "You're dripping water all over my floor."

Ethan sent a last glare at Ammie before he gave Helen an apologetic look. "Yes, ma'am. I'm sorry."

"Is that all you've got to say? I'm still waiting to hear what you're doing standing in Charlotte's parlor at this hour. Is there trouble somewhere?" Helen demanded.

"Yes, Ethan? Is there trouble?" Ammie's voice dripped with a sweetness Ethan knew damn good and well she didn't mean.

"No more than usual, ma'am. And it's taken care of." He shot a warning look to the grinning brunette who'd somehow managed to put a solid six feet between them.

"Well, you can stop 'ma'aming' me. You only do that when you're feeling guilty about something." Helen's gaze shifted between the two of them. "I'll clean up the mess in the morning. Right now we should all get ourselves back to bed. Charlotte and I aren't getting any younger, and all this commotion in the middle of the night is downright disturbing."

"Of course," Charlotte agreed as Helen walked past her. "There's been quite enough excitement for one day. Will you be staying with us, Ethan?"

"No," Ammie instantly said. "He will not."

Ethan ignored her as he smiled at Charlotte. "I'd appreciate that very much." Deciding now would be a good time to put at least part of his plan into action, he belatedly remembered to remove his hat and held it against his chest. "I'd like to stay here with you, Aunt Charlotte, the entire time I need to be in town."

"What?" Ammie gasped.

Charlotte acted as if she didn't hear the loud sounds of protest that her niece was making. "How long will that be, dear?"

Ethan smiled. "I'm not sure."

The older woman let go of her robe long enough to wave away the objections coming from Ammie. "It doesn't make any difference, dear. Family is always welcome." When Ammie let out a snort, Charlotte turned a critical eye toward her niece. "That is hardly the sound a proper lady would make, and whatever is it that you're wearing, Amelia Jamison? It looks like a collection of rags."

Ethan cleared his throat to cover a laugh. Ammie might appear to be both annoyed and embarrassed, but the fact was, it did look like she was dressed in rags. He wondered how she managed to still look beautiful in them, even at this late hour. It had always been a puzzle how Ammie looked perfect no matter the setting or what she had on.

Feeling that itch that always irritated him, Ethan waited silently while Ammie did her best to look as innocent as the angel her aunt probably thought she was. Luckily for him, he knew better. And if he didn't, he had the water still dripping down his neck and back to remind him.

"I had to meet a client, Aunt Charlotte. He prefers this sort of attire."

"That giant man was a client of yours?" Ethan doubted that. He'd known about Ammie's little business, and all this time had been under the impression she was making the social rounds to verify or dispel whatever was floating about in the gossip mill society folks were so fond of.

He'd never even dreamed that that she'd been doing things that would take her out late at night, dressed like a boy, and meeting with men like Slab. He wasn't sure exactly what was going on, but he was going to find out and put a stop to it. He didn't want to be worrying about what she was up to once he'd taken care of the current problem and left on the next stock delivery.

"No," Ammie hissed at him. "He was helping a new client of mine."

"And who was that?"

She sniffed. "My clients' names are confidential, and you don't have any need to know them."

"Have you ever stopped to think that one of your new clients might be this Hawkes, or even the ghost killer?" The thought made Ethan's blood run cold.

She put her hands on her hips and glared back at him. "He's nothing of the sort. My client is a prominent member of society and a friend of Uncle Charles'."

They both jumped a little when Charlotte loudly clapped her hands together. "Children. It's too late for an argument. Now you both get off to bed. Ethan, you can have the room next to Ammie's. If you need anything, bother her, since the two of you seem to be intent on doing nothing but bicker."

She frowned when the large clock in the hallway sounded three soft chimes. "And at such an hour! I declare, I won't be able to budge from my room until the noontime meal."

Mumbling to herself, Charlotte moved off. A moment later the sound of her footsteps clomping up the stairs reached the parlor where Ethan and Ammie still stood, glaring at each other.

He finally let out an exasperated sigh. "She's right. It's late and we're both tired."

"I know I asked you this before, but I guess I'll have to ask again," Ammie said. "What are you doing here, Ethan?"

Remembering Jules pointing out to him that he hadn't actually told Ammie he'd be coming back into town, Ethan rubbed a tired hand against his cheek. "I only had to get some things from the ranch and make sure Luke and Shannon knew I'd be staying in town for a while."

"You don't need to stay if you're thinking about standing guard over us because of what Christine said." Ammie shrugged, making the knee-length coat sway against her slender waist and hips. "Uncle Charles is undoubtedly busy hiring men to do that."

Ethan didn't doubt it, but whoever Charles hired, they wouldn't be good enough. Since he didn't believe Ammie would appreciate him saying that, he settled on something she might agree to. At least until he persuaded her to go stay at the ranch.

"I was planning on helping Jules and Cade track down this Hawkes and his hired gun." He knew he'd been right when Ammie's brow furrowed and she bit her lip. It wouldn't be very easy or wise under the circumstances for her to turn down the services of the best tracker around.

"I also work for John and I'm pretty sure he'll insist on it," he threw in for good measure.

"John's back East," Ammie said in an absent voice. From the way her nose was crinkled up, it was obvious she was still thinking over his offer.

"Charles said John's business is completed, and he's probably on his way back to San Francisco." He held his breath while Ammie remained silent.

She finally looked over at him, the deep turquoise of her eyes turning an even darker shade of blue. "It's a good offer, Ethan."

He nodded, then continued to watch her silently.

Ammie sighed and peeled off the old coat, revealing a

rough linen shirt with leather ties at the neck. Its ends were stuffed into a form-fitting pair of pants tied at the waist with a short length of rope. Ethan tried not to stare at the clear outline of her hips and legs.

"Is that what you wear when you go out at night?"

Giving him a puzzled look, Ammie shrugged. "Since I have it on, I assume you already know the answer to that."

He pointed at her britches. "That isn't right, Ammie."

"What?" She looked down and then back up at him. "They're a little snugger than my other britches, but I can move more easily in these." Her smug little smile was back. "As you found out this evening."

Somehow, that wasn't making him feel any better. But when she lifted a hand to stifle a yawn, he let it go for the moment. She needed rest. "We'll talk about it in the morning."

Ethan gritted his teeth when Ammie stretched her back, pulling the shirt tight across her breasts. When she finally dropped her arms to her sides, she shook her head at him.

"No, we won't. And I'm going to bed. Come along if you want me to show you which room is yours, or sleep on the divan if you'd rather."

Left with little other choice, Ethan followed her out of the parlor and up the stairs, carefully keeping his eyes at a point above her head and not on the enticing sway of her backside. Staying so close to her was going to be a sore test of his control. Repeating to himself that she was family, and in a different layer of society than he occupied, Ethan was glad to reach the far end of the hallway where Ammie waved at a solid oak door as she passed by it.

"This room is yours."

Ethan reached for the handle and had the door half open when Ammie turned and looked at him.

"Ethan?"

"Yes?"

"I'm sorry I yelled at you in the parlor the day my mother was here." She crossed her arms and leaned against the door frame. "I wasn't upset with you as much as I was at her. You were just a handier target."

He relaxed his shoulders and smiled back at her, even though he doubted if she could see it in the dark. "I know, Ammie. I didn't mind. You had to get your anger out somehow. You never could think straight when you were angry."

"Yes, well. Then as a peace offering there's something I want to share with you." She straightened away from the door and dropped her arms to her sides. "Someone else was there when my father was murdered." Ammie spoke so softly that Ethan had to strain to make out the words. "He has to know about Mr. Hawkes and this ghost killer."

Taken by surprise, Ethan took a small step forward before he stopped himself. "Who is he?"

Ammie shrugged. "He'll be here at eight tomorrow morning. You can talk to him then."

She didn't glance his way again before opening the door into her bedchamber and disappearing inside.

8

The sun had been up for a good hour when Ethan left his bedchamber, closing the door softly behind him. Used to ranch hours, he didn't expect to encounter anyone on his way to the kitchen. He wasn't sure when a household of society women started their day, but he figured it was probably sometime closer to noon than dawn.

In all the years he'd known Ammie, he'd never spent the night at her home. He and Robbie had always stayed with Jules, under the watchful eye of his friend's older brother, Cade, and his doctor wife, Abby. But he was used to doing for himself, so a strange house or not, the loud growling in his stomach reminded him he had missed his supper the night before.

After a bit of searching around, Ethan managed to get a large pot of coffee going on the stove. A little more poking about and he found some biscuits in a tin on the counter, along with a jar of gravy and a small crock of butter in the fancy icebox standing in one corner.

He'd heated up what he needed and was sitting down, finishing up his first plate when the door leading into the back hallway opened. Helen walked in, her brows beetled together as she reached over and lifted an apron hanging from one of the hooks against the wall. She kept her stare on the man who'd politely risen when she'd come in, as she tied the apron around her skinny frame.

"I figured that was you clomping around in here. You're the only one in the house that wears those big boots."

Surprised, Ethan looked down at his feet and frowned. Back at the ranch, everyone wore boots. Even here in town all the men he knew wore them, but he'd never paid much attention to what the women wore.

He looked over at Helen's sturdy shoes with leather laces crisscrossing the front. His mouth turned up into a slight smile. He'd almost forgotten about the time in his life he'd preferred a much quieter step and worn laced boots. Sometimes he'd had to tie those heavy shoes onto his feet with a rag or two, but he'd always made sure he found something to walk around in.

"They're shoes, Ethan," Helen's dry tone cut into the prolonged silence. "And a lot quieter than those boots."

"Yes, ma'am."

Her frown made Helen's face look even longer than usual. "The sun's barely up. Have you already done something you feel guilty about?"

"No, ma'..." Ethan stopped himself mid-sentence and grinned. "No, Miss Helen. All I've done is make some breakfast and put on the coffee. I made extra for you and Aunt Charlotte, so help yourself."

"Now, that was nice of you to save me the trouble, Ethan." Helen walked over to the stove and looked over the two pots gently steaming on its surface. "What's this smaller pot for?"

"Water." Ethan concentrated on shoveling the last of his

biscuits and gravy into his mouth. His shoulders slumped inward when he caught Helen's toothy smile from the corner of his eye.

"I'm assuming you put that on for Ammie's tea?"

"I know she favors it over coffee." He might not have ever stayed in Ammie's house, but that didn't mean he hadn't noticed a thing or two about her over the years. Ignoring Helen's chuckle, Ethan kept on eating.

"Yes, she does. Took after her Aunt Lillian rather than Charlotte when it came to that." Helen lifted the half-filled pot and held it over the sink next to the stove. Balancing it in one hand, she used the other to work the water pump. "We'll need more water. Lillian will be bringing Master Kwan by soon, and they both only drink tea, no matter how many years I've tried to get them to see the error of their ways."

"Master Kwan?" Ethan dropped his fork onto the now-empty plate in front of him and half turned in his chair. Since he'd gone out to live on the ranch with Shannon and Luke, he'd only taken occasional lessons with the Chinese fighting master, although he knew Charles and John had practiced regularly with Master Kwan for decades now. "Why is Aunt Lillian bringing Master Kwan here?"

Helen finished filling the pot and placed it back on the stove before she walked over to lift a tray down from a shelf hanging over a long counter. The tray was still in her hands when she turned around and faced Ethan. "Miss Lillian knew Master Kwan long before she introduced him to Charles. Kwan and Cook were close friends, and it was Cook who had Lillian start taking lessons in that Chinese fighting."

Ethan's jaw dropped to his chest. "Aunt Lillian has taken those lessons?"

The housekeeper set the tray down and started arranging cups on it as she nodded. "For many years now. And don't you be rolling your eyes, boy. Our Lillian could put you on your backside quick enough if she had a mind to."

"Uh huh." Trying to envision the petite Lillian struggling to make him budge even an inch had Ethan smiling.

"I've got a mind to ask her to do just that so I can prove it to you," Helen sniffed. "But I'm thinking there isn't any need. You have a way of irritating Ammie enough that she'll probably do it herself before long." She paused and lifted and eyebrow at him. "I can't think why she hasn't done it before now."

"Ammie's taken lessons with Master Kwan?" Ethan rubbed the side of his cheek as he thought that over for a moment. How had he missed that going on over the years?

He knew she'd taken shooting lessons from the aunts. All the women in the family had since they were young girls. But somehow he couldn't get it right in his mind that the always fashionably dressed Ammie had also spent time with Master Kwan.

Ethan frowned. Then again, he hadn't known about her sneaking around the town at night in urchin's rags either. But Ammie? Taking lessons on how to fight by hand? That was something different all together.

It didn't sit well in his gut. It could be dangerous if those lessons gave her a false sense of safety because she actually thought she could take on a full-grown man if she had to. Which might explain where she'd gotten the courage to roam around at night without any more protection than some raggedy boy's garb.

"Stop thinking up new lectures to give that girl and take this tray into the parlor. She'll be in there now."

Still thinking about Ammie's lessons with Master Kwan, Ethan absently got to his feet and walked across the kitchen. "I doubt if she's up and dressed yet. She was out pretty late last night."

Helen glared up at him as she shoved the tray into his outstretched hands. "You both were, as I recall, since you woke me up with all your noise. Being loud's become a habit with you, Ethan Mayes. Yelling at night and then stomping around in those boots in the morning."

Helen waved at the tray he was holding. "Ammie's sure to be awake by now. She always is. And I put her breakfast on that tray too."

"I wasn't yelling and I don't stomp," Ethan grumbled, then held the tray back out to the housekeeper as his gaze swept over the counter behind her. "You forgot her breakfast."

"What are you talking about? It's right there." Helen pointed at a small saucer holding a biscuit with a tiny smear of jam on top.

Ethan stared at it. One biscuit? No one could live on one biscuit.

"Go on, or she won't have time to eat it before Lillian gets here with Master Kwan. And you tell her to let that tea soak a bit more before she pours herself a cup."

Shaking his head, Ethan carried the tray out of the kitchen and down the back hallway. About halfway to the parlor he became aware of the loud ring of his boots against the wooden floors. Gritting his teeth, he slowed his step, carefully putting his feet down to lessen the noise.

Except for the few minutes of silence he'd had with his coffee and breakfast, the morning was turning out to be more aggravating than listening to Tandy shouting orders at him.

When he rounded the corner and stepped into the parlor, he immediately spotted Ammie. Dressed in a frilly snow-white blouse and dark-emerald skirt with a satin sash in a lighter shade of green at her waist, she made a very pretty picture framed against the deep-pink brocade of the curtains as she stood looking out the large window facing the street.

"You're up early."

She turned her head and smiled at him. Ethan's heart rate picked up, but it was such a familiar feeling by now whenever he was around her, he hardly noticed it anymore.

"So are you, Ethan." Her gaze dropped to the tray in his hands. "And you brought tea, I hope, to go along with that coffee I can smell."

He nodded before setting the tray on the low table in between the two divans. "Helen said the tea needs to soak more before you can drink it."

Having delivered the message, Ethan walked over to the fireplace and leaned on the mantel. He studied her while she took a seat in front of the tray and smoothed her skirt over her knees.

There were dark circles under her eyes, and a stray curl of her richly colored brown hair hung along the side of her face, as if she'd been too tired to pull it all back into the ribbon tied at the nape of her neck. "You need to get more rest."

She shrugged as she lifted the plate with its biscuit off the tray. "I got as much as you did."

He watched in silence as she took a dainty bite of biscuit and jam before returning it to the plate.

"And you need to eat more."

She glanced over at him. "Is there anything else? Perhaps you don't like my ensemble this morning?"

"Your what?"

Ammie laughed. "My skirt and blouse, Ethan. Maybe you don't think they're appropriate for receiving a visitor?"

Ethan knew what a lady's "ensemble" was, he just couldn't believe she'd asked him such a ridiculous question. "What you're wearing is fine, and what's that got to do with food and sleep, anyway?"

She sighed and much to his annoyance, set the remainder of the biscuit aside. "Absolutely nothing."

"You need to at least finish that." Ethan pointed at the abandoned plate of food. As small as it was, at least it was something. He frowned when she primly folded her hands in her lap and shook her head.

"I'm not hungry."

"You can't live on nothing, Ammie," he pointed out. Even the stubborn Amelia Jamison couldn't argue with that logic.

"Did you have breakfast already?"

"Yep. A whole plate of biscuits and gravy. And I'm thinking of having another one."

She blinked. "Oh. Well, that's understandable. You are a lot bigger than I am."

He had to agree with that, but it didn't mean she didn't need to eat at all. "Not so much bigger that..." He stopped when she shot to her feet. He'd have backed up a step or two when she crossed her arms and started tapping one foot, but the very solid rock of the fireplace was behind him.

"Did you just say that I'm almost as big as you are?"

"No. I said I wasn't that much bigger than you, but..." He stopped again when her foot tapping got louder and faster.

"And the difference would be what?"

Ethan frowned. He had no idea how another conversation with Ammie had gotten so far from the point he was trying to make. "I'm just saying you need to eat."

"If you think that will make me as big as you, then I might stop eating all together."

"That's ridiculous, Ammie. Now you're acting like a spoiled brat."

"Oh really?"

He rubbed a hand along his cheek. "We don't have time for this. Lillian will be here with Master Kwan any minute, and I wanted to ask you about the visitor coming this morning."

"Master Kwan," Ammie said, the fire dying out of her gaze. "Why did you say Lillian is coming?"

"Helen told me. What about Master Kwan?"

"He's the visitor." Ammie frowned down at the tray as if she'd just noticed the extra cups and saucers.

"Children."

The calm voice had them both turning toward the doorway where Lillian stood with Kwan beside her. The Chinese fighting master was only an inch or so taller than Lillian, with a deceptively slight build, dark eyes, and a long braid of gray hair hanging down his back. Despite the fact he was approaching seven decades on this earth, Kwan still looked the same as he always had to Ethan.

"I see you still carry on conversations that only the two of you understand." Lillian smiled at her niece before turning her gaze on Ethan. "You're here early this morning."

Ammie shrugged. "He never left. Apparently he had to stay over so he could be sure to air his list of complaints."

Lillian turned a questioning look on Ethan. "Really?"

Ethan felt the heat race up his neck. Grateful that Lillian sounded more amused than annoyed, he did the prudent thing and retreated into his usual silence.

The man standing quietly next to Lillian bowed slightly. "You have both always been this way with each other. It is good that some things do not change." His dark gaze settled on Ethan. "Although it is inevitable that most things do. Now that you are grown, Ethan Mayes, you should know that a wise man does not greet the morning sun or his woman with harsh words."

Since his lessons had taught him to never correct the Master, Ethan stuck with remaining silent. Feeling that strange itch again, he rolled his shoulders before remembering to return a bow to his former teacher and politely gesture to a seat on the divan opposite from the one Ammie was standing in front of.

The older man gracefully moved across the room, his light step not making any noise against the thick carpet as he politely waited for Lillian to take a seat before lowering himself onto the cushion next to hers.

As the tension built in the room, Ethan moved away from the fireplace to stand behind Ammie as she settled back onto the divan. She immediately scooted slightly forward and lifted the teapot from the tray.

"Can I offer you some refreshment?" When both guests shook their heads, Ammie replaced the pot and settled her hands in her lap, her gaze steady on the Chinaman. "Master Kwan, a long time ago Cook mentioned that you were there when my father was murdered." She took in a quick breath. "Is that true?"

Ethan frowned when the man shook his head.

"I was not there, Amelia Jamison."

"Oh."

Ammie sounded so deflated, Ethan had to stop himself from reaching out and laying a supportive hand on her shoulder.

"But you told me in your note that you wanted to talk of this, which is why I have asked Miss Lillian to be here as well." Although he sat perfectly still, somehow his whole posture radiated a quiet strength. "I was not there when your father was killed. But I was there when his body was found by your uncle. And I know of his killer."

"You've met this ghost killer Charles talked about?" Ethan asked.

Kwan's gaze didn't stray from Ammie, even as he answered the tracker's question. "I have not met him. But I know someone who did, and he described the man to me."

Ethan's arms crossed over his chest and he automatically braced his legs apart. "Can we talk to this man?"

"He is dead," Kwan said with no inflection in his voice. "At the hand of the one who killed Eli Jamison." He finally shifted his gaze to Ethan. "The only men who have survived a fight with this shadow of death are Mr. Charles and Mr. John. There are no others."

Lillian nodded. "And Charles and John almost didn't live through it. They were both severely beaten. Your Aunt Beth and I will never forget the night they came home."

Ethan sucked in a long breath. "Beaten? Not shot, or stabbed with a knife?" He frowned and then winced at the small sound of distress from Ammie.

The fighting master shook his head. The soft rasp of his braid crossing back and forth against his back was the only noise in the room. "He uses no weapons other than his body. But it is enough. He is highly skilled in our ancient way of fighting. None can defeat him."

Ammie's brow furrowed. "Then how did Uncle Charles and Uncle John get away?"

"Charles managed to shoot him," Lillian said. "Unfortunately, only in the arm. But at least it proved he could bleed like the rest of us."

"Bad luck," Ethan muttered. If Charles' aim had been better, they could all have slept easier.

"How did Papa get mixed up with these men?"

Ethan wondered if Ammie was even aware she'd called her father by the name she'd probably used when he was still alive and part of her very young life.

"Money." Lillian's clipped sentence left no doubt what she thought of that. "The promise of quick and plentiful riches. And it doesn't really matter what Eli's reasons were. He was easy prey for them and paid the price for it." Her gaze gentled as she stared at her niece. "And so did you."

"Easy prey?" The image puzzled Ethan. He'd spent a fair amount of his childhood with Ammie, and had watched her grow up. Those weren't words he'd use to describe her or her Uncle Charles. Even Aunt Charlotte wouldn't be easy to fool for long. Was Eli that different from the other members of his family?

"The choices the man made many years ago make no difference now, Ethan." Master Kwan's tone conveyed the clear message that there would be no more discussion about Eli Jamison. "It is the choices that were made by his adversary that matter now."

Ammie stirred on the divan, moving forward until she was sitting on the edge of the seat cushion. "Why are they important, Master Kwan?"

The elderly man smiled at her. "I began to teach you when you were only a child. We would sit for many hours and talk about the wonders of life. Often I would tell you an old saying that would enlighten you to the thoughts of others. Do you remember this?" When Ammie nodded, Kwan did as well. "Then you will understand when I tell you one now."

"I will try my best, Master Kwan," Ammie said softly.

"One step. One footprint." The Chinese master didn't give any other explanation as he stood in a single fluid movement. "That is the answer to your question, Miss Amelia Jamison." He bowed slightly then turned as Lillian also rose to stand beside him. "I will send word if I hear of this man being seen on our streets again."

"Thank you." Lillian nodded. "I'll walk with you to the door."

Kwan shook his head. "There is no need, my old friend. Stay and talk with your niece until the letter arrives." He turned his head to smile at Ammie. "Your aunt told me about the letter coming today from your grandfather. Remember what I have told you." He bowed again before turning and walking silently out of the room, leaving the three other occupants staring after him.

Ethan unfolded his arms and returned to his position by the fireplace, the sound of his boot steps breaking the silence in the room. "One step, one footprint? What do you suppose he meant by that?"

Lillian's face scrunched up. "I don't know. Ammie was always best with Master Kwan's riddles."

They both looked at Ammie but it was Ethan who asked the question first. "Well, do you know what he meant?"

Ammie kept her gaze on her hands as she smoothed out her skirts. "I'll need to think about it for a while."

Ethan leaned one arm against the mantel and studied her. Ammie always had been the best of them at guessing games, and he sure knew that look on her face. Like the cat who'd caught a bird. He'd have bet another ride on Mudslide that she knew exactly what Master Kwan had meant to tell her.

"Spit it out, Ammie."

Her head came up and she blinked those big, turquoise eyes at him. "I beg your pardon?"

"You know what Master Kwan meant." Ethan raised an eyebrow. "So don't go hiding behind those proper manners of yours and act like you have no idea what he was talking about."

"Manners which you apparently didn't learn at all," Ammie sniffed.

When he remained silent and simply stared at her, she finally rolled her eyes at him. "Fine. It's simple enough. Master Kwan is saying that every step has a footprint that doesn't change."

9

ETHAN RUBBED A HAND AGAINST THE SIDE OF HIS FACE. A footprint that doesn't change? He'd spent a good part of his life tracking animals and men, so that wasn't much of a revelation as far as he was concerned. Thinking there must be more to it than that, Ethan frowned. "So Master Kwan is saying that this ghost who bleeds after all is going to keep on killing? That isn't much help."

Ammie wrinkled her nose as she shot him an exasperated look. "Honestly, Ethan. That isn't what he meant at all."

"Oh? Then maybe you could explain it to me?" Ethan cocked his head to the side and waited.

Imitating his move by also tilting her head to the side, Ammie matched his stare with one of her own. "I don't believe he was referring to the ghost killer at all. I think he was talking about..."

She broke off, turning slightly to stare at the open parlor door. Ethan's gaze went in the same direction at the sudden burst of noise from the front entryway. Charlotte appeared in the doorway, her shoulders shaking with laughter.

"It seems we have quite a bit more company." She

wagged a finger at Ammie. "How many people did you invite to be here when this letter arrives from your grandfather?"

Her niece got to her feet and smiled sweetly at Ethan. "I didn't even invite everyone who's here now."

Knowing good and well she was referring to him, Ethan barely had time to roll his eyes before the room began to fill up. He couldn't stop the smile when Ammie let out a small shriek and lifted her skirt high as she dashed across the room. In barely a second she was engulfed in a three-way hug with her two good friends, Dorrie and Brenna.

Since it would be impossible to be heard over the joyful chatter of their reunion, Ethan looked over the heads of the women and nodded to the two men who had strolled in behind them. Jules returned his nod while Robbie flashed the easy-going grin that had let him wiggle out from under most punishments when the three of them had been growing up together.

The women were talking so fast that Ethan couldn't understand a word they were saying, but that was certainly nothing new. Dorrie and Ammie had done the same thing all the years they'd been growing up together, and when Brenna came along and married Robbie, well, she'd fit right in, making the same fuss and engaging in the same conspiratorial whispers as the other two.

Which had been a puzzle for Ethan.

He never recalled his sister, Shannon, acting like that whenever she got together with the rest of his honorary aunts. He glanced over at Charlotte and Lillian who were talking quietly together, as if to prove his point. He'd have to ask his brother-in-law about that. Ethan grinned. Whenever they had absolutely nothing else to discuss.

After a few minutes, Charlotte clapped her hands

together. "Ladies. I suggest we take this to the kitchen where I'm positive Helen is waiting for us with some refreshments, and we can have a nice, cozy chat at the table."

She smiled at Ethan. "And you can offer the men something a bit stronger from the brandy cart." Charlotte waved in the general direction of the far side of the parlor before she and Lillian herded the younger women out the door.

"Since you're going to be in the kitchen, eat something," Ethan called out as Ammie and her friends disappeared out the doorway. Her faint, "no", had him grinding his teeth in frustration.

Jules raised an eyebrow at this friend. "You seem to be making yourself at home here."

"Well, if you're now the man of the house, I'd like a whiskey," Robbie chuckled. "It was a long ride yesterday." He paused as he looked from the empty doorway back to Ethan. "I guess Ammie didn't eat her breakfast?"

"What?" Ethan frowned.

"Her breakfast," Robbie said slowly, emphasizing each syllable. "She usually eats a biscuit for breakfast." At Ethan's hard stare, his grin grew wider. "At least she did every time I stayed here." Robbie looked up at the ceiling. "It was fine since I'm an honorary cousin and considered family and all."

The tracker's eyes narrowed. "Just what room did you stay in whenever you were here?"

Robbie's blue eyes twinkled in amusement. Every inch as tall as his two friends, but leaner with much lighter hair, the rancher had the classic good looks that had always attracted the women and been the reason for a lot of good-natured ribbing from his friends.

"The one at the top of the stairs." He wiggled his eyebrows at Ethan. "Which room are *you* in?"

"The one Charlotte told me to sleep in," Ethan grumbled. He gestured toward the cabinet against the far wall. "I don't know if there's any whiskey but help yourself."

Jules shook his head. "It's early yet for me. I still have work I need to get to later on."

"I don't, so I can have a drink while I'm waiting to hear where you're sleeping," Robbie said. "And I'm also wondering if Cook knows that you're staying here? You do remember him? The man who considers Ammie his granddaughter?" When Ethan remained silent, Robbie went cheerfully on. "Or how about Charles? That would be her uncle?"

Ethan crossed his arms and glared at his friend. "What are you doing here, anyway? Don't you have a ranch to run?"

"Dorrie sent for Brenna, and since I'm married to the woman, where she goes, I go." Robbie laughed. "See how that works?" He shrugged. "We also were due for a supply run."

"Why did Dorrie send for Brenna?" Ethan demanded.

"Same reason Brenna couldn't have stopped me from coming along even if she'd tried. To see you finally have to deal with Ammie." Robbie backed up a step but kept the grin on his face. "In case Jules hasn't told you yet, when she has you going to the tea shop and to Maggie's place, you may as well roll over and play dead. You're hogtied."

Ethan's back stiffened. "What are you talking about?"

Jules held up a hand. "Stop poking at him before you end up in a brawl right here in Charlotte's parlor and I have to haul you into jail." The marshal walked over to one of the divans and sat down, placing the hat he'd been carrying on the table in front of him. "Dorrie said that letter is supposed to arrive this morning."

Robbie's smile instantly faded as he followed Jules and

settled into a chair. "This sounds like a nasty business, Ethan."

"I know it." Ethan ran a frustrated hand through his hair. "This Simeon Hawkes and his ghost killer is likely headed this way. For all I know, they could already be here."

"I'm surprised Charles and John let the man get away all those years ago," Jules said quietly.

Robbie shifted in his chair. "They were more concerned about Ammie. I remember when her mother left."

Ethan straightened away from the mantel and dropped his arms to his sides. "You do?"

The rancher shrugged. "Sure. Ammie was about six years old then, as I recall. I was staying at The Gentleman's Club with Lillian, Cook, and Helen when Charles was courting Lillian. It was the same time his brother was murdered and Christine Jamison returned to New York. I remember hearing them talk about it before they realized I was listening to every word they were saying."

"What was Ammie like back then?" Ethan asked. When both men stared at him, he hastily added, "I mean, was she really upset about her mother leaving?"

Robbie sighed. "Didn't seem to be. But then she took to Lillian like a duck to water. I went to live on The Orphan Ranch a few weeks after that, so I only saw Ammie whenever Lillian brought her out for a visit." He slumped down in his chair. "I always regretted that. I should have gone into town and checked on her. Lillian offered to bring me back with her more than once. I usually said 'no' until the two of you showed up in the family. I liked it on the ranch and didn't even think about Ammie."

Ethan's shoulders relaxed. "Since Jules and I came along only a couple of years after that, she wasn't in town alone very long. And she had Dorrie here to keep her company."

"Which might not have been a good thing," Jules said with a grin. "Those two of them together used to get into a heap of trouble."

"Still do." Ethan shook his head. "And Brenna's no help."

"My wife's as stubborn as the other two when it comes to that," Robbie agreed. "What do you think is going to be in that letter?"

"I don't know." Glad to focus on the immediate problem, Ethan stared at the floor for a long moment. "Master Kwan seems certain that everything is going to be repeated."

Even from his position by the fireplace, Ethan could see Jules' entire body tense. "What does that mean? We're already sure this ghost would kill again."

"Or maybe they're both going to come after another Jamison." The thought had Ethan's blood turning into ice.

Robbie's fingers drummed against the arm of the chair. "I didn't realize that they'd come specifically for Eli Jamison."

"I doubt if they did. It's likely that he was just the convenient target who came along," Jules said. "But I haven't heard the whole story from Charles yet."

"Neither have I," Ethan admitted. "But I'm tending toward agreeing with you. But I haven't figured out how it fits with what Master Kwan said."

"What did he say?" Robbie asked.

"One step. One footprint." Ethan shrugged. "He didn't tell us what it meant, only that it was the answer to Ammie's question."

Jules leaned forward and rested his elbows on the top of his knees. "What did Ammie ask?"

Ethan was quiet for a moment while he thought back to Master Kwan's visit. "She wanted to know why the choices that her father's killers had made were so important."

Robbie snorted out loud. "And how does 'one step, one footprint' answer that?"

"I don't know." Ethan blew out a short breath. "But Ammie does."

"What did he mean?" Dorrie frowned at her friend, her brown eyes reflecting the worry in her voice.

"That Hawkes and his assassin won't change. They'll make the same choices again." Ammie gave a decisive nod even as Brenna and Dorrie exchanged a confused look.

"You mean to lure someone with the promise of money and then kill them?" Brenna chewed on her lower lip. "Why would they do that?"

"They were thieves, Brenna," Lillian clarified before shifting a serious gaze to her niece. "I see what you and Master Kwan are saying. That it isn't only what they will try to do, but how they will do it as well."

Ammie nodded quickly, smiling at her aunt's quick grasp of what the fighting master had been telling them. "I believe so. However they approached Papa before, they will try the same thing again with someone else." When Lillian gave her a skeptical look, Ammie's brows drew together. "What?"

"I'm not at all sure that would work this time. Hawkes' scheme became well known in society since he tried to dupe several young men besides your father. Including young Milton."

Young Milton? Ammie blinked. She'd just been hired to follow a young Milton. But Aunt Lillian was talking about something that had happened twenty years ago.

"That wouldn't have been Nathan Milton, would it? Did he need more money for gambling debts?"

Her eyes snapping open, Lillian stared at her niece. "How did you know that? Have you met Nathan Milton?"

Thinking that an apple really didn't fall far from its tree, and ever mindful of the absolute discretion she always promised her clients, Ammie nodded as she picked up her teacup. "Society isn't so large that I wouldn't have met one of the city's more prominent merchants."

"Who happened to tell you he had a gambling problem in his youth?" Lillian shook her head. "It isn't important. What we should be talking about is that if Simeon Hawkes tried the same thing again, he'd be recognized."

"But it was so long ago, Aunt Lillian," Dorrie protested as Charlotte and Helen began to chuckle.

"There's still plenty of us around after twenty years, girl," Helen said. "I've met the man, and I'd recognize him if I saw him again. Even if he hasn't got one hair on his head and a paunch that sticks out over his belt, I'd still know him."

"What does Ethan say about this, dear?" Charlotte asked.

Ammie shut her eyes. Why should Ethan have any say in it? It wasn't his problem, so he'd likely be riding off again in the very near future. With a sigh, she opened her eyes and focused on her aunt. "Ethan thinks they're coming back to kill me."

Her bald statement had everyone around the table but Lillian gasping in shock.

"Could he be right?" Dorrie looked around as if she expected someone to leap out at them at any moment.

"Of course not," Ammie scoffed. "Since he decided that was the reason they're coming back to San Francisco, he's obsessed with the idea."

"I wouldn't say he was obsessed, Ammie." Lillian's voice was laced with amusement. "He's simply very protective of you. He always has been."

Ammie ignored the nods around the table. "Well then, he has a very strange way of showing it since he's never around to protect much of anything." She frowned into her teacup. "And for someone who isn't home much, he has a lot of odd notions about me."

Brenna laughed. Her mouth curved upward in a generous smile as she looked at her friend. "Are we talking about the same man whose eyes light up every time you come into a room? That Ethan?"

The brunette put her forearms on the table and leaned forward. "They're sparkling with annoyance, not pleasure, Brenna. The man has nothing but complaints." She pursed her lips. "Just today he told me I was fat."

"No!" Five voices protested in unison.

"Has he gone blind?" Dorrie demanded. "Two of you could fit into a pair of his britches." She cast a sideways glance at Charlotte. "Not that you would ever, ever do such a thing, of course."

"Of course not, dear." Charlotte sent Dorrie a shaming look before turning her attention to her niece. "I'm sure you're exaggerating, Amelia. I can't imagine Ethan saying such a thing."

Ammie was certain that he hadn't really meant that she was fat, but she still had every intention of standing her ground on this. He was getting entirely too bossy, and she'd really enjoy hearing Ethan get a stern lecture on manners from Charlotte or Lillian. Preferably both. "And when I protested, he called me a spoiled brat."

Her very glamorous aunt laughed. "Now that I can believe, Ammie, since he's called you that on a number of occasions through the years." She lifted an eyebrow at her niece. "And most of the time it was well deserved."

"Well I don't think he has any call to say you're fat or a spoiled brat," Brenna stated, making it clear where her loyalties lay.

"Me either." Dorrie curled an arm around Ammie's shoulders in a solid show of support.

Feeling grateful to both her friends, Ammie nodded and then froze when the tall clock in the entryway chimed out the hour. She slowly counted each one. They stopped at ten chimes. The time the messenger had sent word that he'd be calling on her.

Everyone held their breath as footsteps echoed down the hallway toward the kitchen. A moment later, the door swung open and Charles poked his head around its edge.

"I came up the front steps with the messenger from Eli's father-in-law."

Charlotte rose first, reaching over for Ammie's hand and drawing her up as well. "Ammie, dear, you and Lillian go on with Charles. The rest of us will wait here." She looked over at her younger brother standing in the doorway, waiting for his wife to join him. "And you send the other husbands in here to wait for the news with us. There are things you might want to explain to Ammie that are best for her to hear first."

10

THE MESSENGER HADN'T HAD MUCH TO SAY. TALL AND THIN, with wings of gray hair growing back from his temples, he'd handed her the plain, cream-colored envelope with a slight bow. He'd declined her offer of refreshment, and after another slight bow, had wished her a good morning and vanished out the front door. Ammie stared after him for a moment, acutely aware of the weight of the letter in her hand and the three pairs of eyes staring at her. Knowing there was no help for it, she slowly made her way to the divan and sat down. Her aunt and uncle were seated across from her, and Ethan stood in his usual spot next to the fireplace.

With a sigh, Ammie broke the elaborate seal on the envelope and drew out the single sheet of paper. The ticking of the clock on the desk in the corner filled the room as Ammie silently read through the first words she'd ever had from a grandfather she'd never met. When she'd reached the bottom, her gaze skipped back to the top to stare at the first two sentences.

Dear Granddaughter, I hope this finds you well. I'm writing to inform you about the man who killed Eli Jamison.

She was still staring at them when she heard her uncle shift his weight.

"Well, Ammie? What did the old bastard say?" There was no mistaking the impatience in Charles' voice.

Ammie raised her eyes to his and forced a smile onto her lips. She'd have to sort out her own emotions later. Right now there was a more urgent problem to deal with.

"The old bastard said that your hired man is following the wrong lead." Ammie's expression softened when her aunt laughed. When Lillian winked at her, Ammie's inner turmoil subsided into a weight in the pit of her stomach. When she finally turned to look at her uncle, there was more than a touch of her normal cockiness in the eyebrow she raised at him.

"Your hired man? Would that be Uncle John?" From the corner of her eye she caught the hard stare Ethan shot at Charles. It appeared the expert tracker hadn't known what John's trip back East was about either. Somehow that little tidbit of knowledge made her feel better.

"It's time, Charles," Lillian said quietly. "Ammie needs to know."

Ethan braced his legs apart. "She needs to know what?"

Catching Ethan's gaze with hers, Ammie shook her head at him then waited until he settled back on his heels again before returning her attention to her uncle.

"I believe you have something you need to tell me?" She smiled when her uncle looked down at his boots. "I promise I won't fall apart."

Her uncle's head snapped up. "I know you won't." He stood and stepped around his wife to pace toward the parlor door and then back again. Stopping a few feet away from where Ammie sat quietly watching him, he looked down at his niece and ran a hand through his hair. "I've spent a good many years protecting you from them."

"From them?" Ammie echoed. "Who are they, Uncle Charles? My mother? My grandfather? The man who killed my father? Or does your list also include Papa?"

Charles' mouth dropped open as he continued to stare at Ammie, his dark-brown eyes turning almost black in what Ammie knew was a sure sign of a spiking temper. But feeling the weight of the letter in her hand, Ammie's spine stiffened. This time she was not going to let her loving uncle back away from the truth to spare her feelings.

Taking a deep breath, she calmly stared back at him. "I've always known what mother was like." She cut a quick glance at the letter clutched in the hand lying in her lap. "And now this grandfather as well." Returning her gaze to her uncle, she tilted her head to the side. "Right after we all chased my mother out of the house, you mentioned that Papa had gone looking for laudanum? I've spent enough time with the doctor in the family to know that it's used for pain. Why did Papa have to go looking for it?"

Charles made a rough sound in his throat as a tic showed along his hardened jawline. For a moment, Ammie wasn't sure he was going to answer her question until his shoulders drooped and he shook his head. "Eli was a fine man, Ammie, and a good father and brother. But when he suffered an injury on the voyage here, one of our fellow passengers gave him a bottle of laudanum. Even after we landed and his ankle was healed, Eli couldn't stop taking it, and it changed him."

Lillian reached up and clasped her husband's hand before turning a sad look to Ammie. "When the doctor wouldn't give him any more, he went looking elsewhere for it. Hawkes was with him the last time he sought out the medicine.

"It was the same night your father had emptied his bank account," Charles said, taking up the narrative again. He sat down next to his wife on the divan. "I found out from Nathan Milton that Eli had been investing in Hawkes' scheme of locating a sunken treasure ship, although I have no idea how Eli thought they could recover the treasure, even if they did know where this supposed ship went down."

Ethan moved away from the fireplace to stand behind Ammie. "So you believe that when your brother and Hawkes went to find the laudanum, Hawkes had this ghost killer of his follow them and murder Eli for his money?"

Ammie heard the crackle of the letter as she tightened her hand around it. Tucking away what she'd just learned about her father, she frowned at the two people sitting across from her. "And what does all this have to do with Uncle John?"

Charles shrugged. "We know Hawkes and his man got on a ship sailing to New York. So John has kept his ears open for any murders over the years that sounded like the ones Hawkes' man had committed here. A couple of times John's men got close, but never close enough. And over the last five years the trail has disappeared."

"Until recently?" Ethan prompted.

"That's right," Charles confirmed. "We got word of a man making the rounds in the social circles of New York trying to find investors for a sunken treasure. With the new railroad opened up, John thought he'd go check on it personally."

"All these years," Ammie breathed. "All these years you've been looking for Papa's killer?" She looked down at her lap. "And my grandfather has been too." She lifted her chin slightly as she held the letter out to her uncle. "Here."

Reaching over and gingerly taking the letter between two fingers, Charles smiled at his niece. "Thank you, but I know that you'll tell me everything that in it." He set the letter onto the low table between them. "And now I have a feeling *we* will be looking for him."

"No."

The single word came from over Ammie's head. She twisted in her seat to look up at Ethan. "Yes. But you don't have to, Ethan. I'm sure you have other plans."

Ethan's eyes narrowed on her face. "We'll talk about it later."

Ammie shrugged. "Fine." She turned back around to face her uncle. "The letter said that Uncle John was following the wrong lead, and that Hawkes' old associate is no longer with him." Ammie leaned over and tapped a slim finger on top of the letter lying on the table. "He also said that Hawkes has engaged several other such associates over the years."

"So the odds are in favor of this ghost killer being dead?" Ethan said.

When Ammie looked over her shoulder, he smiled at her and added "good".

"I'd agree with that." Charles nodded. "What else did Christine's father say?"

"Something interesting." Ammie settled back into her seat. "That reliable rumors, and yes, that's exactly the way he said it. That reliable rumors claim this newest associate moves easily in society, and even Mr. Hawkes is afraid of him." She stared at her uncle. "And that Grandfather's men confirmed Mr. Hawkes bought two train tickets for San Francisco."

Ammie turned in her seat again and looked up at Ethan. "They left a week ago.

Ethan leaned forward. "Which means he's already here."

~

HALF AN HOUR LATER, Ethan frowned at the three people sitting on the divans. He didn't like where this discussion was going. Not one bit.

Ethan had gone back to his usual position in front of the fireplace. His arms were folded over his chest as he stared at Charles. The man could not seriously be considering allowing his niece to take part in the hunt for this Hawkes person.

"If he's here, *I'll* find him." Ethan nodded when Ammie stopped in mid-sentence and all three turned to stare at him.

"How do you propose to do that, Ethan?" Ammie challenged. "You don't know what he looks like, or even when he arrived in San Francisco."

"I'll find him," Ethan stated again. And he would. No matter what it took. "I'll start at the train station. One of the agents might remember him. All I'll need is a description."

"That's fine, Ethan," Lillian said. "I recall the man very well. He was a normal height. I'd say more on the shorter than taller side. He had brown hair, brown eyes, and a very slight English accent, although he may have lost that after all these years." Ammie's aunt smiled. "And he always dressed very well."

"Brown hair, brown eyes, an average kind of height." Ammie pursed her lips. "Excellent. Ethan shouldn't have any trouble at all tracking Mr. Hawkes down."

"I'll go around to the hotels." Ethan's jaw set into a stubborn line.

Ammie threw her hands into the air. "It's still the same description that could fit hundreds of men. And you have no idea what name he's using."

Lillian nodded her agreement, a light-colored curl swaying against her cheek. "I doubt if he'll use 'Hawkes' again. His face and the name together might trigger an old memory in someone he comes upon by chance."

"He never stayed in a hotel," Charles said. "He stayed in a house."

"He'll likely do the same thing again," Ammie said. "One step. One footprint."

Frustrated, Ethan rubbed a hand against the side of his jaw. "You'd think with all his money, this grandfather could have discovered something more solid for us to use."

"We do know how he goes about his scheme, if he keeps to the same pattern," Lillian said. "He looks for someone to dupe in the ranks of society." She gazed off to a distant point. "I remember how he told me about the society parties he'd attended, and whenever he was in The Gentleman's club, he would spend all his time talking with my wealthiest customers."

Charles lifted her hand to his lips and placed a kiss on the inside of her wrist. "Not all of his time, sweetheart. I recall him fixing his attention quite a bit on you."

"It was no secret that I had built up some wealth of my own."

Charles smiled at his wife. "And beauty. I'm not sure which attracted the man more, but he definitely felt he had a claim on you."

Wealth and beauty? Ethan glanced over at Ammie who was watching her aunt and uncle. What had she said about one step, one footprint? That it meant Hawkes would repeat all his previous actions. It made that itch of his erupt to hear the kind of woman Hawkes targeted fit Ammie so well. She certainly had a close connection to a good deal of money, and there simply wasn't a more beautiful woman in the city.

"Which is why he's found an associate who can move easily in society," Ammie said slowly. Her forehead wrinkled as she stared down at the letter from her grandfather. After a moment, she glanced over at Lillian. "As you said, he can't risk being recognized, so he won't be able to go to the functions. But according to that letter, his associate should have no problem being accepted into society's best parlors."

A trickle of relief ran down Ethan's arms. He nodded at Charles. "Then all you have to do is go to the parties and find some newcomer who's looking for money. He should latch onto you soon enough. Let me know who he is, and I'll track him back to this Hawkes person and take care..." Ethan broke off when Charles started shaking his head.

"It's a good plan," Ethan insisted.

"It could be," Charles said. "But Lillian and I don't attend the parties regularly and haven't for a good many years." He leaned back and stretched an arm out along the back of the divan behind his wife. "We cause too much of a disturbance at those things."

"Sadly that's true," Lillian said with a smile that showed she was anything but upset about it. "And because we don't attend many of society's gatherings, I doubt if we would know who has recently arrived in town without asking around, which might scare off this new partner that Hawkes has taken on."

"But I go to the gatherings quite regularly," Ammie declared.

Ethan closed his eyes and gritted his teeth. She could not be serious.

"It will be easy for me to spot anyone who is new."

"No."

She airily waved Ethan off. "Yes. And I believe we've already had this one-word conversation." She stood and put her hands on her hips. "And I might remind you, Ethan Mayes, that you have no say in how I spend my time, or where I choose to spend it."

He took a step forward, his arms once again crossed over his chest to keep himself from reaching out and shaking some sense into her. "You're part of my family and that gives me a say, and I say you aren't going to any parties to make yourself a target where a killer might be roaming about."

"Oh really?"

"Children." Lillian clapped her hands together. "I don't know why lately you two always end up in an argument." She pointed at Ethan. "We need to find this man, and Ammie is right. She can make an appearance at the parties and no one would think it was out of the ordinary. And the odds are very good that she can spot who we are looking for much quicker than any of the rest of us." When Ammie sniffed, her aunt shifted her finger to point at the younger woman. "Ethan is also right. You come from a wealthy family and would make an excellent target."

Ammie's shrug had Ethan fixing a hard stare on her.

"There is a problem, though," she admitted. "I usually attend the functions with Aunt Charlotte, and I don't want to put her in any danger."

"You'd do better with an escort along," Lillian agreed.

Her niece smiled. "I'll ask Adam. I'm sure he'd be delighted."

Ethan stiffened as he stared at Ammie who had pointedly turned her back toward him. Who was Adam?

"Also an excellent idea," Charles put in. "But not who I had in mind. You'll take Ethan with you."

Ammie frowned as she shot Ethan a sideways look. "No."

"Yes." Ethan took a step forward until he was directly in her line of vision. He wanted to be sure she'd heard him.

"We aren't going to get into this again, are we?" Charles muttered under his breath. He sighed when he met Ammie's glare. "You'll take Ethan with you because I know he can shoot."

"We aren't going to be shooting anyone in the middle of a party, Uncle Charles," Ammie argued.

Ethan snorted at that. "I will if I have to." He deliberately smiled when Ammie turned her glare on him. "But don't worry. Your friends will be safe enough. I hit what I aim at."

Ammie's beautiful eyes narrowed. "So do I, Ethan."

That made him chuckle. "Only when you're using that special-made rifle of yours, and I can't see you toting it to a party under your skirts."

"I will if I have to," she shot back, in a perfect imitation of him.

"Family is better, Ammie," Charles said quietly. "I'll know who to soundly thrash if he doesn't protect you properly."

His niece rolled her eyes and Ethan snorted at either notion. He couldn't imagine letting anyone, not even an honorary uncle, give him a whooping, and he certainly would never fail at protecting Ammie. Hell, he'd been doing that for a good part of his life.

"All right, then it's settled," Lillian declared, breaking into Ethan's thoughts.

The beautiful woman he'd adored ever since she'd become a substitute mother in his eyes, rose from the divan, smoothed her skirts out, and smiled at him. "You'll need proper clothes. We can have some of Charles' altered quickly. I'm sure Maggie will help."

Maggie was Jules' mother-in-law and owned a dress shop in town. Remembering Robbie's words, Ethan had no intention of spending any time in her establishment. He'd felt awkward and completely out of place the few times he'd been dragged inside, and since he'd been grown, that was only once. When Jules had been chasing after Dorrie before she'd agreed to marry the marshal.

"Fine," Ammie said grudgingly after a long pause. "I still need to go over to The Lick House and let Christine know that we'll take care of this problem." When her aunt and uncle looked taken aback by her announcement, Ammie shrugged. "I promised her I would stop and see her after the letter from her father arrived."

Charles and Lillian exchanged a quick look. "She left two days ago," Charles said. "I've had a man keeping an eye on her hotel, and he reported back to me that she got on the early morning train headed east."

Ethan immediately shifted his gaze to Ammie. For a long moment she sat perfectly still. It didn't even look to him as if she was breathing. He'd already taken a step toward her when she slowly stood up.

"Well. That's good. It saves me paying a call I wasn't looking forward to." Ammie leaned down and scooped the letter off the table, carelessly stuffing it into a pocket hidden in the seam of her skirt. "I know we still have a few details to work out, but I didn't get much sleep last night. I think I'll lie down for a while."

Laying a hand on her husband's shoulder, Lillian

nodded her understanding. "That sounds like a good idea, Ammie. Would you like me to come up and sit with you for a bit?"

Ammie shook her head. "No. I'm fine. If you'd make my apologies to the others, I'd appreciate it."

"Certainly." Lillian gave Ethan a warning glance when he opened his mouth.

He frowned as Ammie made her way out of the room, quietly following her far enough so he could watch her climb the stairs. When he turned back, the frown was still on his face.

"Is something bothering you, Ethan?" Lillian asked.

"Just one thing." Ethan looked at the empty doorway and then back at Lillian. "Who's Adam?"

11

An hour later, Ethan was bidding Charles a good night, but his mind was still on the image of Ammie walking up the stairs, her steps dragging and her head down. As the gambler headed out to the front porch to enjoy a cheroot, Ethan joined his friends standing at the other end of the entryway, watching their wives.

The women were gathered together in a tight circle near the front door as they said their goodbyes to Lillian. From many hours of experience, Ethan knew it would be a while before Lillian would actually get out the door, so he stood between his friends and settled in to wait.

It only took a minute before Robbie leaned slightly toward him and whispered loudly enough for Jules to hear. "If you have any more questions for the marshal about this plan of yours to flush out Eli Jamison's killer, you'd better ask them before our wives demand that we don't talk to you anymore."

Ethan gave Robbie a puzzled look. "Why would they do that?"

When Robbie only grinned at him, Ethan looked over at Jules. "Well?"

The marshal kept his eyes straight ahead as he shrugged. "You might have annoyed the women."

Ethan's brows snapped together. "I haven't even talked to them. What have they got to be annoyed about?"

"Fat?" Robbie sounded as if he was about to burst out laughing. "You called Amelia fat?"

Ethan shot an annoyed look toward Ammie. "I did not."

Now Jules leaned to the side as he kept his gaze on his wife. "Dorrie says you did. And that you also called Ammie a spoiled brat."

"I've called her that before."

Robbie chuckled softly. "You also named your horse Brat." He looked around Ethan and grinned at Jules. "Do you think he ever told Ammie that he named his latest mare after her?"

"I doubt it," the marshal said.

Ethan rolled his eyes to the ceiling. "My horse has a mind of her own and acts up at times. I didn't name her after anyone."

"Uh huh."

Robbie's skeptical tone had Ethan gritting his teeth. The last thing he needed was for his friend to tell Ammie that he'd named a horse after her.

"She's used to you calling her brat," Jules whispered. "But I'm thinking that you saying she's fat might have hurt her feelings some."

"I didn't call her fat. You only have to look at the woman to know that." Exasperated, Ethan dismissed the whole notion. "You fix it with your wives. I haven't got time to deal with this nonsense right now."

"You fix it with Ammie first, and that will fix it with our

wives," Robbie said. "And you'd better be quick about it, because Lillian's left and they're headed our way."

Ethan shut his mouth and smiled at Dorrie and Brenna. Both women only gave him a cool look before turning to their husbands.

"I'm going up to check on Ammie before we leave." Dorrie rose on her toes and placed a quick kiss on Jules' cheek. "I won't be long."

"Uh huh." Jules grinned when his wife frowned at him. "Take your time, honey. We aren't done yet lecturing Ethan on his poor manners."

While Ethan mentally throttled his friend, Dorrie beamed at her husband. "An excellent idea."

"I'll join you," Brenna said.

She also leaned in to give her husband a quick kiss on the cheek, but Robbie quickly turned his head so her lips landed on his mouth. When she pulled back and gave him a reproving look, he only winked at her which had her smiling back at him.

"You might want to help Jules with his talking." Brenna looked over at Ethan and shook her head. "It might take a bit for Ethan to come around."

As the women made their way up the stairs, Ethan reached out and gave both his friends a firm push. "You say one word and we'll be breaking a few pieces of Aunt Charlotte's furniture."

Robbie clapped him on the back. "Since that would probably have me sleeping somewhere besides my own bed, you won't hear a word from me about your strange way of charming a woman."

Jules smiled. "I'm going to have to agree with Robbie on that, Ethan. You do have an odd way with Ammie."

Ethan scowled at him. "I don't treat her any differently than I do any other woman."

"Which explains why you sleep alone every night." Robbie grinned but took a long step backward when Ethan gave him a hard stare.

All three men turned at the sounds of footsteps descending the stairs. Dorrie reached the bottom first and hurried over to Jules, wrapping a hand around his arm as she turned troubled eyes on Ethan. "Ammie's not here."

Ethan stared back at her. "What?"

"She's not in her room," Brenna said. "And her rifle's gone too." She nodded when Ethan frowned. "I know where she keeps it."

Dorrie stepped in front of the tracker who was also her childhood friend. "She wasn't so upset by the letter from her grandfather that she'd go out looking for this Mr. Hawkes on her own, was she?"

Ethan was silent for a moment as he thought that over. No. It wasn't the talk about her papa's murder that had upset Ammie. She'd already had several days to get used to that. But it was the first she'd heard about Christine leaving without another word to her daughter.

"I have an idea where she is." Ethan gave Dorrie's shoulder a brief pat. "I'll find her."

As the two women walked arm and arm into the parlor, Ethan let out an exasperated snort. "Making sure she stays safe would be a whole lot easier if Ammie told me where she was going."

Jules clapped a large hand on Ethan's shoulder. "I've found that it helps if you ask someone to do that."

Pushing his friend's hand away, Ethan turned on his heel and headed for the door, plucking his hat off a hook and settling it firmly on his head.

He heard the shots long before he reached the edge of the line of trees that surrounded the secluded cove with its wide beach. It was the favorite place for the women in the family to get away from town for a while, and to practice their shooting.

The three young boys had discovered it by following one of their aunts long ago. Of course, they'd also been spotted by that same aunt, and their spying had resulted in a long list of added chores for several weeks afterwards. But he hadn't minded doing them. It had been worth it to find out where Ammie spent her time whenever she disappeared with her aunts.

Now he watched her from the edge of the trees as she methodically shot at a row of small rocks she'd placed on one of the logs strewn along the sand. Pieces of rock exploded upwards as the shots came in one continuous flow. Ethan was both surprised and proud of how accurate Ammie's shooting was. He had to admit that she hadn't been simply trying to annoy him when she'd said she hit what she aimed at.

Watching her, he had to wonder if maybe she was just a slightly better shot than he was. Dismounting from Brat, he walked a few steps closer and considered the matter. She was good. But then hitting a moving target, not to mention one that was breathing, was a much different thing than shooting at rocks. He was inclined to think that Ammie wouldn't be able to pull a trigger when it came to shooting a live man.

And she certainly would never shoot a woman, no matter how much she was likely imagining doing that very thing right at the moment.

"You might as well come out, Ethan. Unless you enjoy lurking about in the trees."

She'd surprised him again, spotting him in the shadows like that. Leading Brat out into the open, he walked slowly across the mixture of dirt, rock, and hard-packed sand on the upper part of the beach. As he drew closer, he dropped the reins. Brat immediately halted and lowered her head to the tufts of grass growing in small patches here and there.

Ammie stood watching him, her rifle held against her side with the barrel pointing at the ground. She was dressed in a pair of plain brown britches and a dark-blue shirt tied at the neck. She looked every bit as feminine as she did in her most elaborate gowns. Ethan reacted to the sight with his usual frown.

"Are you following me?"

Since he'd made it a habit of always telling her the truth, he nodded. "Yep."

She sighed heavily and shook her head. "Well. At least you aren't lying to me."

"Like your mother did?" Ethan asked quietly.

Ammie's shoulders stiffened before she turned and lifted her rifle to her shoulder. "She isn't my mother. But yes. Like her."

Ethan waited while two more shots rang out and the last two rocks lifted high into the air. When Ammie stood there, not moving, he stepped closer until he could lay a hand on her shoulder.

"You're right. She isn't your mother. Lillian is. So anything Christine says shouldn't bother you."

He felt her shoulder slump beneath his hand.

"No, it shouldn't. But it does." Ammie broke the contact when she abruptly turned around. "I told her I would come see her after the letter came. And she nodded. I saw her. Even knowing she wouldn't be there, she still nodded."

Ethan could feel her pain as if it was his own. "Lying comes easily to women like Christine."

"You mean beautiful women, with money and nothing to do with their time but cause problems."

The bitterness in Ammie's tone had Ethan treading softly with his words. "You aren't like her, Ammie."

She gave a short laugh. "No? Aren't you the one who calls me a spoiled brat?"

"That's different."

Ammie rolled her eyes before she turned her head away to look at the open water of the bay. "Oh really?"

Ethan stared at her averted face. Since he was twelve years old, and she'd been eight, he'd always known what she was feeling, sometimes even when there was a hundred miles between them. He knew Ammie was hurting, but he didn't understand why. After all, Christine hadn't been part of her life for a long time, and Ammie had never even mentioned her over the years. Ethan had always assumed she had little or no memories of her mother. So why was she so angry now?

Thinking he may as well start with the obvious, he kept his voice low and gentle. "I didn't know you even remembered your mother."

"I remember her." When Ethan remained silent, she let out a deep sigh. "The truth is, I remember being carried around by Uncle Charles more than either of my parents. Especially on the ship when we came to San Francisco." She sighed again. "My most vivid memory of my parents is the anger in their voices whenever they spoke to each other. And I remember the day Christine told me she was leaving, and I would be staying with Uncle Charles and Lillian."

She turned to face him. "I wasn't the least upset by the news then. And I only have flashes of Uncle Charles telling me about Papa being killed. So, what does that mean, Ethan? That I act just like her?"

Ethan dropped both hands onto her shoulders, holding her gaze with his. "You aren't anything like her. You care about people, about the family. You know that."

When she didn't say anything, he tightened his grip. "I'm sure you'd have a very different reaction if Lillian told you she was leaving. Or your uncle. And remember how you were when Dorrie disappeared, or you thought Robbie wasn't treating Brenna right, or even now, trying to protect Charlotte from any danger." When the corners of her mouth turned up a little, he nodded so she'd be sure to know that he meant what he was saying.

"I remember, Ethan. You don't have to squeeze me into believing it."

He immediately lightened his grip but kept his hands where they were. He needed to keep that connection with her.

She continued to stare up at him, chewing on her lower lip. It was obvious that there was something she wanted to say, and Ethan was willing to stand there all day until she did.

"I don't know anyone else whose mother chose to leave her child behind."

Ethan's hands dropped away from her shoulders in sheer surprise. "What?"

Ammie stood straighter and lifted her chin a notch. "My mother chose her life in New York over me. And my father didn't choose me either."

Completely confused, Ethan's brows snapped together. "What did your father do? Besides get himself killed?"

"Exactly," Ammie said. "He emptied his bank account and went looking for that medicine. How was he going to provide for a child? Did he give me a thought at all when he did that, or when he went looking for laudanum that night?"

Her lips compressed into a thin line. "Would *you* have done that?"

Ethan blew out a breath and rubbed his hand along his cheek. She was right. It had not only been a foolish thing to do, but a selfish one as well. "No." He hesitated, picking his words carefully. "A lot of us in the family don't have our blood kin with us. Both of my parents are dead."

"Cook told me your mother died in childbirth." When Ethan frowned at her, Ammie shrugged. "I asked him about her a long time ago. And your father died too, which is why Shannon adopted you as her brother."

He smiled slightly at that. His father was dead now, but he hadn't been when Shannon had a paper drawn up claiming him as part of her family. "More or less. But my point is that you aren't the only one with no parents."

"But mine didn't die, Ethan. They chose a life without me."

"Your father died."

Ammie shook her head. "He'd already made his choice."

"While a lot of others chose to stay with you. Like Lillian, Charles, Charlotte, and even Cook and Helen," Ethan pointed out.

"I know. And I am grateful." She looked away. "It's just hard to be a throwaway child that my parents didn't care enough about to stay with." She seemed to huddle further within herself. "It always makes me wonder how many others look at me the same way."

Ethan placed a finger under her chin and gently turned her face back toward him. Those beautiful eyes that haunted his dreams at night and dogged him every day he was on the trail, were misted over with tears. Acting on pure instinct to soothe her pain, he lowered his head and brushed his lips against hers.

Nothing had ever prepared him for the electric shock followed by a wave of heat. Unable to do anything else, he pressed his mouth down on hers, sliding his fingers along the graceful curve of her jaw and lifting his other hand until he was cradling her face between them while his lips moved against hers. When her mouth opened and her arms slid around his waist, he was lost. Ethan kissed her with all the pent-up longing of every long year since he'd first laid eyes on her.

He held her face to his, keeping it there as he pressed his tongue deep into her mouth, exploring every inch. It wasn't until his own growl of pleasure penetrated the haze around his brain that he forcibly drew his head back, violently breaking their kiss and leaving Ammie breathless and staring up at him with a dazed look in her eyes.

Speechless, Ethan took a very long step back, putting as much distance between them as his long legs could manage.

"I'm sorry."

"Sorry," Ammie repeated, still staring at him as she took a small step forward.

Ethan quickly retreated, holding one arm out to stop her if she came any closer. "Stay put."

Ammie blinked once and then again, finally giving her head a quick shake. "Sorry? Did you say that you're sorry?"

Lost in his own guilt, Ethan didn't hear the growing anger in Ammie's voice. "We're family. It was a mistake to kiss you like that. It isn't right." Not used to the powerful emotions warring inside him, Ethan crossed his arms over his chest and almost growled at her. "You were crying,"

"So you kissed me because I was crying?"

He kept his arms firmly locked down as he glared at her. "I just wanted you to stop."

Now Ammie's hands came up to her hips. "Is that how you stop any woman you see from crying?"

Even knowing the big hole he was digging for himself, Ethan shrugged. "Sometimes." When her face turned bright red, he hastily reached for something else to say to keep her from exploding. "We can't get into another tussle, Ammie. You know we can't. We can do that after we catch Hawkes and his partner."

"Which I don't need you to do, Ethan," Ammie snapped out. "I can assure you that Adam can shoot just fine."

Not exactly in the mood to hear her talk about another man while his whole body was still on fire for her, Ethan scowled. "Maybe he can. But I doubt if he can track."

Ammie sniffed at that. "I don't know. I'll have to ask him."

"We're doing this hunt together, Ammie, or you won't be doing it at all."

"Oh really?" She turned on her heel and stomped off toward her horse who was grazing peacefully further down the beach.

He braced his legs apart and watched her go. "Yes, really. Either I'm going to that party with you, and anywhere else we need to go until Hawkes is caught, or I'm putting you over my saddle and taking you out to the ranch until it's safe," he called after her.

Ammie reached her horse and took her time gathering up the reins and climbing into the saddle. He half expected her to take off at a gallop, but she surprised him when she walked her mount over to where he was still standing, arms crossed over his chest and staring at her.

"You can't make me go anywhere, Ethan. And despite what you think, I'm not helpless or stupid. Adam might know how, but he still wouldn't be the best tracker around." She paused before spitting out, "you are. And I want my father's killer caught, so that means we'll need to do this together."

Relieved he wouldn't need to spend hours arguing with her, Ethan nodded.

"But that doesn't mean I have to like it." She pursed her lips when his eyes narrowed on her face. "And if you're going to keep from being barred entrance to these parties, I suggest you work on your manners. You simply cannot go about kissing every woman who looks upset. And you can't make unflattering comments about their appearance either." She turned her horse and set the animal into a trot toward the trees.

"I did not call you fat," Ethan yelled after her, rolling his eyes when she ignored him and kept riding on. When Brat lifted her head and turned large, liquid brown eyes in his direction, he scowled at his horse. "I didn't say she was fat."

Ethan stood and listened until the sounds of Ammie's departure faded away into the air. He took his hat off and slapped it against his upper thigh. There were two things he was certain of. Ammie was going to make him crazy before they managed to catch Hawkes. And once they did, he was going to leave for a stock delivery. He didn't care where or for how long, but now that he'd kissed her, there was no way he could stay.

He was still that street urchin who'd stolen and lied whenever it had pleased him. As sure as he was standing there, already wanting her back in his arms, Ethan knew he wasn't good enough for her. And like Shue had told him long ago, he couldn't change where he was from or who he was. And neither could Ammie.

12

Three days later, Ammie was still brooding as Helen firmly pinned the last burnished curl into place.

Stepping back, the long-time resident of the household looked over her work with a critical eye before breaking into a toothy grin.

"You're as beautiful as our Lillian was at your age." She reached over to gently push a stray hair away from the back of Ammie's neck. "And every bit as smart, which is more important, Ammie. And don't you be forgetting that."

"I won't, Helen," Ammie said automatically as she leaned forward and gave her image in the mirror her own assessment. Helen was only being kind. Ammie could see for herself that she'd never hold a candle to her Aunt Lillian.

The fact was, she looked exactly like her mother.

Knowing how her Uncle Charles felt about his former sister-in-law, Ammie wondered how he'd been able to stand looking at his niece all these years. Making a face at herself, she leaned back and caught Helen frowning at her.

"What's wrong?" Ammie glanced back at her image, searching for an uncooperative curl.

"I might be asking you the same thing," Helen said. "You've been acting funny ever since you got back from your shooting practice." She nodded when Ammie only blinked at her. "I saw you go sneaking out with that rifle of yours. I also saw Ethan go chasing after you."

"Ethan?" Ammie did her best to look as innocent as she sounded, and knew she'd failed miserably when Helen laughed.

"Yes, Ethan. And don't try telling me that boy didn't find you."

"Oh, he definitely found me," Ammie groused.

Helen smiled. "And got your back up, as usual."

Ammie shrugged. "He does have a way about him."

"He's worried about you, Ammie. We all are." The housekeeper raised one hand when Ammie started to protest. "I know you think it's your aunt and uncle who are more of a threat to Hawkes. And that could be true since I'm sure he hasn't changed much, and he was a man who enjoyed taking revenge for any harm done to him. But the black cloud I see is hovering over *you*, not Lillian or Charles. So Ethan is right to worry." Helen picked up a wrap that matched the deep green of Ammie's gown. "And men do strange things when they're worried."

They most certainly do, Ammie thought, but she kept her lips firmly pressed together in a smile, simply nodding as she rose from her seat in front of the mirror. Helen could talk all night if she had a mind to. Ammie was still put out with one Ethan Mayes.

And more specifically at his apologizing for a kiss that had been everything and more than she'd ever dreamed it would be. But clearly it hadn't meant anything to him. The man had acted as if he couldn't wait to break it off, and then compounded that insult by apologizing and declaring that kissing her had been a mistake.

"What are you huffing about?" Helen demanded.

Startled, Ammie quickly shook her head. "Nothing. I'm just anxious to get to the party, is all."

"I don't see why. You never much liked them before," Helen said as she continued to straighten out Ammie's skirt, and brush a hand over the back of her bodice.

"I have clients I need to talk to, and this will be a good opportunity to do so. With everything that has happened in the last few days, I'm afraid I've been neglectful. I wouldn't want them to think poorly of Inquiries."

Which was true enough. She still had to report back on young Milton's leisure activities to his father. Remembering the night that William Milton had had to be carried home also brought up the picture of Ethan flailing about in the water, sputtering as she... Ammie froze. She not only saw the tracker in the water, but in her mind she could hear him as well, yelling out at Slab. Ethan had called the big man by his name. He'd known who Slab was.

Ammie's foot began to tap as she carefully went over the events of that night in her mind. Yes. She was sure Ethan had said Slab's name.

"*Now* what are you riled up about?" Helen asked. She'd stepped back and was frowning at Ammie.

"I need to ask Ethan something. Is he downstairs?"

"Of course he is. Where else would he be since he's staying here?" Helen softened her words with a smile. "And he's looking very handsome in that nice suit Charles gave him."

Not doubting that for a minute, Ammie swept out of the room and down the hallway. It only took her a minute or two to reach the parlor doors. She was already several steps inside before she spotted Ethan on the far side of the room, holding a whiskey glass in one hand as he listened intently to something Jules was telling him. Both men looked over at her, but it was Jules who stepped forward first.

The marshal raised his eyebrows and let out a low whistle, making Ammie laugh. She drifted down into a graceful curtsy to acknowledge his unspoken compliment.

Rising, she gifted him with a bright smile. "Thank you, sir."

She glanced over at Ethan who saluted her with his glass before raising it to his lips and taking a sip. Ignoring him, Ammie turned her smile back onto Jules. "I wasn't expecting to see you here this evening."

"I wanted to go over the plans with Ethan." Jules jerked a thumb over his shoulder. "I thought that our friend there, who apparently has no idea how to act around a beautiful woman, needed to be reminded that if he does spot our man tonight, to only follow him, and not do anything foolish."

"If *we* find him, Jules, I'll be sure to keep your advice in mind." Ammie had no intentions of allowing Ethan to go charging after anyone without her.

Jules grinned. "You'll have to work that out with Ethan."

"We already have," Ammie assured him.

The marshal looked at Ethan and grinned. "Is that a fact?"

Charlotte bustled into the room, beaming when she spotted Ammie. "You look wonderful, dear. As always." She moved forward and slipped an arm around her niece's waist before glancing over at the two men. "Isn't she lovely?"

"Yes, she is," Jules said while Ethan silently nodded. The marshal's smile grew wider. "It's a pure wonder why any of those society men bother to look at another woman." He shot a foot over and prodded the toe of Ethan's boot. "Isn't that right?"

When all Ethan did was glare at his friend, Charlotte clucked her tongue at him. "Where are your manners, Ethan? You'll never get along in society if you simply stand about like a stone statue."

"I'm not looking to get along in society," Ethan grumbled.

"Well, you'll need to until this business is taken care of," Charlotte declared. "And since you are not only Ammie's family escort tonight but also her chaperon, you'll need to be mindful that no young man tries to take any liberties."

Ethan set his glass down on a table with a hard thump. "Have any tried before?"

"Of course." Charlotte's airy assurance was followed by a careless wave of her hand. Completely oblivious to the dark look Ethan shot at her niece, Charlotte smiled at Ammie. "But she's always turned them away. Maybe tonight she'll meet one she won't want to turn down."

Used to Charlotte's always-hopeful assurances that the perfect man would darken their doorstep at any moment, Ammie laughed and winked at her aunt. "I'll be sure to keep my eyes open, Aunt Charlotte."

"Of course, dear. I have no doubt." Charlotte gave Ammie's cheek a gentle pat before handing her a long pair of gloves. "I had these laundered for you."

Ammie nodded her thanks as she pulled them on and called out to her obviously reluctant escort for the evening. "Are you ready, Ethan?"

He stepped forward and pointed to the open parlor door. "Let's go."

Wishing he wasn't so absurdly handsome in his dark suit

coat and matching trousers, Ammie sailed past him, leaving a faint scent of jasmine in her wake.

She picked up a package wrapped in cloth and tied with twine that was lying on the small table in the entryway, then stopped at the front door and gave Ethan a pointed look. She patiently waited until he'd yanked it open, and then brushed past him without a word.

Ammie smiled to herself when she heard Jules laugh, and her mood lightened even more when Ethan pulled the door shut with a loud bang. Suddenly, she felt much better about the evening.

Stepping up to the carriage that the stableman had brought around to the front, Ammie smiled at the young man as she accepted his help into the cozy space inside. While Ethan walked around to climb into the driver's seat, Ammie placed her package into the small space behind her and settled her skirts to keep them away from Ethan's boots.

Her escort took up the reins and set their horse into motion before glancing over at her.

"What did you bring?"

Ammie continued to fuss with her skirts, finally ignoring his question in favor of asking one of her own. "How do you know Slab?"

He frowned. "What?"

She eyed him in exasperation. "I know your hearing is excellent, Ethan. I asked you about Slab. The night you took a swim in the water trough, I distinctly heard you call him by his name."

"I was pushed into that trough, and I know a lot of people in town. Slab is too big to miss for long." Ethan casually held the reins against an upraised knee as he kept his gaze on the street. "I'd be interested in hearing how it is that *you* know Slab?"

"As you said, he's too big to miss." When Ethan shot her an annoyed glance, Ammie shrugged. "He's an associate of mine at Inquiries. We work together quite often."

"Is that a fact?" Ethan said, borrowing one of Jules' favorite phrases. "Are there any other of these associates I might be running into?"

"Quite a few," Ammie admitted. "But most likely Mouse and Wang Wei."

"Wang Wei?" Ethan turned in his seat to face her. "Master Kwan's grandson? That skinny little kid we used to go fishing with on occasion?"

Ammie smiled at the picture of Ethan, Jules, Robbie, and Wang Wei casting their lines while standing on the edge of one of the shipping piers. "He's not a child anymore. Although he is still rather thin."

"And who is Mouse?"

"One of the former orphans at Lillian's ranch. He and Wang Wei are close friends. Mouse works for Cook at The Crimson Rose."

Ethan grunted. "When he isn't working for Inquiries?"

"That's right."

With little more to say, and reminding herself that she was still angry with that apology he'd given after their kiss, Ammie fell silent and wasn't at all surprised when Ethan did the same. Neither spoke another word until he pulled the horse to a stop in front of the Lewis' home near the top of Nob Hill.

"Nice view from up here." Ethan nodded toward the bay that was sparkling in the moonlight.

"Yes, it is," Ammie agreed as she gathered her skirts around her. "Although I do like it better later in the evening, when the fog is coming onto shore."

"It always made a nice cover."

Ammie gave him a puzzled look. It was an odd thing to hear from a man who spent so little time in town. Since he was already climbing out of the carriage, she didn't have a chance to ask him about it before he appeared next to her, his hand held out to help her down. He offered a rare smile once she was standing securely next to him.

"I used to wonder why women bothered with all those skirts. Seems like a lot of trouble to me. But I've come to appreciate them."

Taken by the unusual teasing note in his voice, Ammie couldn't help but smile back at him. She always did have to work hard at staying mad at Ethan. "Why is that?"

"It gives men a chance to hold their hands." He winked at her before turning his attention to the young boy who'd seemingly appeared out of nowhere to see to their horse and carriage.

Ethan reached into his vest pocket and produced a gold coin, holding it directly out in front of the boy's wide-eyed stare. "This is yours if you keep the carriage nearby." Ethan pointed to a spot near the walkway that was already occupied by a closed carriage. "There's another gold coin like this one if I come out and find our carriage right there."

The young boy looked over at the other conveyance and then back at Ethan. "Looks like a good spot for it, sir."

The two grinned at each other in perfect understanding while Ammie raised a gloved hand to cover her smile. Ethan really could be quite charming when he wanted to be. Too bad it wasn't very often.

As they made their way up the walk toward the tall mansion, painted all in white with long columns along its front, Ethan drew her hand into the crook of his arm. He looked down at her as they climbed the steps up to the wide veranda that spanned the entire length of the house. "You never told me what was in that package you put into the carriage."

Tilting her head to one side, Ammie politely returned his smile. "A change of clothes in case we have to follow someone."

When he rolled his eyes, she withdrew her hand from his arm and nodded at the footman who was holding open the front door for them. Stepping in ahead of Ethan, Ammie paused for a moment to remove her wrap and hand it to the servant standing in the grand entryway with its high ceiling. Both the front parlor and the larger room across from it were filled with the evening's guests. Ammie inclined her head to the room on the right.

"Let's start in there. I'll introduce you to a few people, and then I'll make my way to the other room while you stay and look over the guests in the parlor."

Ethan frowned at her. "Ammie, I'm not sure that's a good idea."

She ignored him and tugged on his arm to get him moving. "Of course it is. Come on, I see Adam and Christa. We'll start with them."

Practically dragging him behind her, Ammie started to thread her way through the parlor, finally catching the eye of the petite honey-blond, who enthusiastically waved back at her. Christa immediately gave the tall man with the piercing blue eyes standing next to her a poke in the side with her elbow before moving off in Ammie's direction. The two women met halfway across the room, greeting each other with a warm hug.

"How are you?" Christa asked. "It seems ages since I've seen you."

Ammie laughed. "It *has* been ages. At least two weeks."

The man who'd followed Christa across the room shook

his head. "Closer to one week since I distinctly recall being roped into escorting you both to the door of Maggie's shop." He quirked an eyebrow at Ammie. "I've been hearing some very interesting whispers about you lately."

"Which he has refused to share with me," Christa declared. She peered around Ammie. "And who is this? I know it isn't Jules or Robbie. This can't possibly be the elusive Ethan, can it?"

Well aware that Ethan did not like being singled out, Ammie glanced over at him and almost giggled when a streak of red crept up the back of his neck. Not feeling the least sympathetic, she looked back at Christa and nodded. "It most certainly is."

Christa's tall companion smiled slowly as he held out his hand. "I'm Adam Fromer, and this chatty nuisance is Christa. It's good to meet you at last." He shook Ethan's hand as he studied the man. "Ammie tells me that you're an expert tracker."

Ethan inclined his head at the compliment. "And you're Christa's husband?"

Adam gave Ethan a bland smile. "No. Sorry. I'm her brother. And I understand you and Ammie are family of sorts as well? You're considered cousins?" His smile grew deeper at the abrupt nod and stony stare he got in return.

Sensing a spike in Ethan's temper, Ammie didn't bother to try to figure out why, she simply turned a bright smile on Christa as she stepped around her friend to slip her hand through the obligingly raised crook of Adam's arm. "Christa, would you be kind enough to introduce Ethan to a few of the gentleman and ladies while I talk to Adam? We have some business to discuss."

Christa laughed. "Oh, you two always have business to discuss, but I'd be very happy to stroll about the room with your handsome cousin." She smiled when Ammie's eye's narrowed slightly. "You go on with Adam and take your time talking over whatever it is that always so fascinates the two of you." She stepped up and latched onto Ethan's arm, leading him off as Ammie stared after them.

"A problem, princess?" Adam's amused voice was low and close to her ear.

"Of course not," Ammie said as she continued to stare after Ethan and Christa. When they were swallowed up by the crush of people in the room, she looked at Adam. "And don't give me that smirk, Adam Fromer. I have something important to tell you."

"Does it have anything to do with my hearing that you have an older twin who has mysteriously come and gone from The Lick House?"

Resigned to Adam always knowing everything that went on in the city, Ammie smiled at him. "As a matter of fact, it does."

13

Ethan took a quick glimpse over his shoulder and frowned. He and Christa were completely surrounded by other guests, so he'd lost sight of Ammie. Which had brought that itch again to the back of his neck. He also hadn't liked the familiar and easy way Adam Fromer had led her off — as if he'd done it a dozen times before. Made him wonder just what else Fromer had done with Ammie.

"Hello?"

Ethan blinked when Christa waved a hand in front of his face.

"It's very rude not to pay attention to the lady you're with, Mr. Mayes." When Ethan shifted his gaze to her, she smiled at him and pushed a tightly curled ringlet away from her face. "Of course, I'm no Amelia Jamison, but I've been told I'm pleasant enough company."

Feeling the heat rise up his cheeks, Ethan searched around for something to say. He never had been much good at talking to women. Except for a few. And those are the ones he'd grown up with.

"I'm sure your conversation is fine," he got out, then frowned when she laughed.

"Why, I simply can't remember when I've had such an honest compliment."

The light note in her voice had Ethan's shoulders relaxing a little.

"I haven't heard you talk much," he offered, thinking he might need to explain what he'd said.

"Well then, we must rectify that." She tugged enough on his arm to get his feet moving. "I'm supposed to introduce you around, but perhaps we should start out slow?"

Not at all sure what that was supposed to mean, Ethan followed her lead. It only took a minute before Christa came to a halt right behind a gentleman who was bending over a pot filled with tall plants. Ethan peered over the stranger's shoulder. It looked as if the man were closely examining a clump of dirt he held in his hand.

Christa reached over and tapped the man in the center of his back. "Henry. I have someone I'd like you to meet."

"What?" Henry swiftly straightened up and twirled around as flecks of the dirt he still held in his hand spewed out around him. As if he'd suddenly realized what he was holding, Henry quickly tossed the dirt in the general direction of the pot and held out his hand.

Ethan slowly brushed small pieces of soil from the front of his vest and coat before staring down at the man's grimy hand.

"You should wipe your hand off, Henry," Christa patiently instructed, then smiled when Henry dutifully rubbed his hand against his dark trousers, leaving a noticeable streak down the side, before holding the slightly cleaner appendage out once again.

Christa nudged Ethan in his side. "This is Henry Fromer. My other brother."

Since it wouldn't have been the first time his hand had been covered in dirt, Ethan reached out and shook Henry's as the younger man blinked rapidly behind a pair of gold wire-rimmed glasses.

"Henry, this is Ethan Mayes. He's a part of Amelia's family," Christa said, finishing the introduction.

Brother and sister definitely shared a family resemblance with their hazel eyes and honey-blond hair. Henry's was thick and looked to be in constant danger of cascading over his glasses. He was as tall as Ethan, although a bit leaner, and the tracker was surprised at the strength in the man's grip that was at odds with the bookish look about him. Ethan smiled.

"Are there any other brothers I'll be meeting?" At Henry's blank stare, Ethan inclined his head toward Christa. "Your sister has already introduced me to Adam."

"Oh?" Henry's gaze bounced around the room. "Where is he?"

"Off with Amelia, discussing secrets as usual."

Discussing secrets? Ethan shot Christa a questioning look, but she only smiled sweetly at him.

"Ethan? Did you say Ethan?" Henry frowned. "You're Amelia's tracker?"

"What?" Ethan's frown was a match for Henry's. "I'm not Amelia's anything."

"Yes, you are," Christa said cheerfully. "I'm just not sure what, though, since there are so many possibilities." She cocked her head to the side and studied him. "Just a cousin? A potential husband? Prison guard, maybe?"

Ethan's arm jerked. "Prison guard? Amelia said I was her prison guard?"

Christa laughed. "Perhaps 'prison' is too strong a word. But you do threaten quite often to lock her in her room, don't you?"

"Not on a regular basis," Ethan grumbled, although the idea did have its merits.

"You have a ranch, don't you? And a stable and stock business here in town?" Henry blurted out.

Distracted, Ethan turned his head toward the man who now had his hands clasped behind his back and was rolling up and down on the balls of his feet. "My brother-in-law, Luke does."

"Excellent. I'd like to stop by and examine the stock and their feed supply."

"Why?" Ethan was genuinely puzzled. Who examined feed unless an animal got sick?

Henry leaned forward, his expression serious. "You can think of it as a hobby of sorts. Do I have your permission? At the end of the week would be convenient." He nodded before hastily adding, "of course I'll send you a note the day before to be sure I still have your permission."

His curiosity aroused, Ethan slowly nodded. "All right. I don't think Luke would mind, as long as I'm there to keep an eye on you."

"Wonderful." Henry stuck his hand out again and grabbed one of Ethan's, giving it several enthusiastic pumps before releasing it to adjust his glasses and sweep a thick clump of hair away from his eyes. "I need to see to a few things." He started off then turned and walked backwards for a few steps. "I'm delighted to have met you."

When Christa's brother plowed into a group of loudly protesting gentlemen standing close by, Ethan shook his head with an amused smile. It stayed in place as he watched Henry make a hasty apology before disappearing into the crowd near the parlor door. Ethan grinned. He liked Henry a lot more than he did the oldest brother, Adam.

Which conjured up a mental image of the tall imposing man smiling down at Amelia as he'd led her away. *Lamb to a slaughter,* Ethan thought as he stretched his neck in an attempt to stare over the heads of the mob of people in the room.

"Are you going to tell me who you and Amelia are looking for?"

Ethan's attention snapped back to Christa. "What?"

"Amelia is clearly looking for someone, or she wouldn't have grabbed Adam so fast to find out what he knows." At Ethan's stare, Christa gave a delicate shrug. "My brother has the odd talent of knowing everything that goes on in San Francisco." Her lips quirked and a sparkle came into her eyes. "Well, almost everything. He and Amelia often exchange information." When Ethan remained silent, Christa pursed her lips. "And now she's brought along her elusive tracker."

Her silent companion weighed his words for a moment. Ethan wasn't sure how much Amelia would want confided to her friend, but he saw no harm in having another pair of eyes searching the guests. "We're looking for someone who recently started attending the society functions."

"How recently? The town is growing fast, Ethan. We have newcomers to our little society almost on a daily basis," Christa pointed out.

He frowned at that bit of information. It wouldn't make their search any easier.

"In the last week, maybe two at the most." Ethan hesitated, thinking over what Charles had said. "He might show a particular interest in Ammie."

Christa rolled her eyes. "The last week or so would

narrow it down some. But showing a particular interest in Ammie? It would be simpler to find a man who didn't show an interest in her." Once again her head was cocked to the side. "Or haven't you noticed how beautiful your cousin is?"

"I've noticed," Ethan conceded through gritted teeth. "She also has a tendency to get into more mischief than she can handle."

"Ah. Then you're here as a guard *and* a tracker." Christa had the pleased look when someone learns a closely held secret. When he retreated into silence once again, Christa sighed. "Amelia hasn't been to any of the functions in the last week or two, so if whoever you're looking for is here tonight, this is the first time he would have seen her."

Alarmed at the thought, Ethan twisted at the waist, looking for the fastest route to the door leading into the room Ammie and Adam had disappeared into.

"Why yes," Christa said to the back of his head. "I do think it would be an excellent idea to go keep an eye on her. From a distance, of course, in case we can spot someone who is taking an unusual interest in her."

"Excuse me?"

Since Christa's voice had come from behind him, Ethan reluctantly turned around.

"William!" Christa dropped her hand away from Ethan's arm as if it had been scorched, and smiled at the newcomer.

The man was positively beaming back at her, and Ethan didn't need a pair of Henry's glasses to see that he was completely taken with Christa. Not knowing who the stranger was, and feeling somewhat responsible for looking after Ammie's friend, Ethan sighed and held out his hand.

"I'm Ethan Mayes."

The slightly shorter, dark-haired man with the boyish

features stared back at Ethan with his mouth slightly open. "The tracker? Amelia's tracker?"

"Cousin," Ethan corrected. "I'm her cousin. And you are?"

"Oh, sorry." The man reached out and gave Ethan's hand a quick shake. "I'm William Milton. And I apologize. I didn't realize you had a blood connection with Amelia."

"Not blood," Christa put in cheerily. "Something Ammie's tracker should keep under careful consideration."

"I'm not..." Ethan started to deny before clamping his mouth shut when Christa cut him off.

"As a matter of fact, Ethan was just going to desert me to go in search of Ammie."

Ethan gave a mental snort at that bald-faced lie, and then another one when Christa batted her eyelashes at the besotted-looking William Milton, who of course came to her rescue. A circumstance that Ethan was sure Christa had been maneuvering for.

"We certainly can't have that," William declared. He executed a short bow in Ethan's direction. "I'd be happy to keep Christa company while you go looking for your... um... cousin."

Christa stepped closer to a grinning William and placed a gloved hand lightly on his sleeve. "That's a wonderful solution." She turned to glance at Ethan. "William and his father are close friends of the family, so I'll be fine in his company."

Ethan's mouth twitched at the little minx's smug grin. "A good friend of the family, is it?"

"Why, yes," Christa said airily. "Rather like a cousin not by blood."

"Funny." Ethan's eyes narrowed. "Behave yourself. And stay in this room."

"Or you'll lock me in mine?" Christa laughed at Ethan's glare. "Go find Ammie. Just in case there actually is someone who's taking an untoward interest in her. And ask Adam as well. He'd notice such a thing."

Thinking he just might find a private place to talk a number of things over with Adam Fromer, Ethan nodded at the couple staring back at him. Feeling that was adequate enough to take his leave, he turned on his heel and threaded his way toward the door. It took him several minutes, and a firm push or two, before he could make any headway into the room on the opposite side of the wide entryway. It was even more crowded than the parlor.

Ethan stood inside the doorway, getting his bearings, before turning to his left and heading for the fireplace built into the far wall. He was still ten feet away when he heard a burst of male laughter coming from a group just off to the side.

Glancing in that direction, he stopped dead and narrowed his eyes on the flash of green satin in their midst. There was only one woman who would attract that kind of attention. Ethan carefully looked over the group, searching for the man who was supposed to be at her side as he escorted her about.

Annoyed that Adam, for all his polished manners, seemed to have deserted Ammie, Ethan started to look around the room when he felt that itch again. Taking a slow, deep breath, his gaze returned to the group surrounding Ammie. It only took him a few seconds to spot the man standing just on the outside of the circle, his hands clenched into fists at his sides.

He was barely an average height, but had a solid build. And there was something unnatural in the way he held himself completely motionless as he stared into the center of the group. He could have been looking at anyone with that intent concentration, but the itch on the back of Ethan's neck told him it was Ammie who was holding his interest.

"First time I've seen the man." Adam's deep voice was low and came from slightly behind Ethan. "The truth is, I wouldn't have noticed him now if he weren't so fixated on Ammie."

Ethan grunted at that, but kept his attention on the man who had inched closer to the edge of the group. "You don't know him?"

"No," Adam admitted. "Which is unusual. He must be very new in town." He stepped forward until he was standing right next to Ethan. "I knew almost the minute Christine Jamison Aldrin arrived at The Lick House, and when she left." At Ethan's sharp sideways glance, Adam shrugged. "My point is that I haven't heard anything about a man named Hawkes, or about this man who's suddenly shown up in our small society."

"No one's perfect, Fromer."

Adam chuckled softly. "But I take offense at anyone coming into my world when I know nothing about him."

Ethan looked over and held Adam's hard blue stare. "I'm assuming you're going to do something about that."

"Of course."

When Ethan shifted his gaze back to the strange man, Adam did as well.

"You can't be in two places at once, Ethan. So I suggest we both do what we do best. I'll find out about our mystery visitor, and you protect Ammie."

"I intend to," Ethan said under his breath.

"That's good," Adam responded as if he'd heard what Ethan had said. "I'll be in touch."

With his attention concentrated on the dark-haired man

intently watching Ammie, Ethan felt rather than saw Adam leave. It was barely a heartbeat later that the stranger suddenly turned and stared directly at Ethan. Not looking away, Ethan didn't even blink as he slowly braced his legs apart and crossed his arms over his chest.

The other man showed no reaction but turned away, his attention once again back on the small group surrounding Ammie. A few seconds later, he was gone.

Ethan kept his eyes on the group as a grim smile tugged at the corners of his mouth. Ethan had seen the man make his escape. Charles' ghost killer might have been untrackable, but this one wasn't.

If that man was the one they were looking for, then Ethan would find him.

14

"Didn't expect to see you again so soon, but I'm glad you stopped by."

Jules settled into a high-backed chair that was covered in a deep, rich brown leather. His personal study was simply furnished, with a desk and two overstuffed chairs for any visitors. A couple of side tables and a built-in bookcase served as the only other pieces of furniture in the room. Several large windows made up the entire wall behind his desk, ensuring the study was always flooded with light during the day.

"Ammie insisted on visiting Dorrie." Ethan shifted slightly to settle more comfortably into his chair.

Jules' blue eyes took on a glint of amusement. "Wasn't that Christa who came in with you?"

Ethan had been a little wary about Ammie's insistence that they stop and collect her friend first before heading to Dorrie's house. The fact was, he'd deserted Christa at the gathering the previous evening, and hadn't thought to check on her again before he'd escorted Ammie home. He knew that if any of the aunts caught wind of his shabby behavior, he'd be in for more than one lecture on manners. Luckily for him, Shannon and Luke were still out on the ranch so weren't likely to hear about it.

To his pleasant surprise, Christa had greeted him with a cheery "good morning", not seeming to be put out with him at all. Which was a good thing since Ammie was still keeping her distance, and he didn't want to have to deal with two irate women.

On the ride home last night, he'd asked Ammie if she'd ever noticed the short dark-haired man who'd been lurking on the edges of the group surrounding her. After a negative shake of her head, all she'd asked was if Adam had also spotted him before falling silent for the rest of the way home. And this morning Ammie had barely nodded a greeting before taking her biscuit up to her room. She hadn't appeared again until the time they'd agreed on to leave for Dorrie's house.

Pushing aside his growing frustration over Ammie's silence, Ethan reached over to the coffee pot that Jules' housekeeper had brought in and left on the desk. Pouring out a generous mug for himself, he looked over its rim at his friend who cocked an eyebrow at him.

"Robbie said to tell you to be careful," Jules said.

"Did he and Brenna head back to the old Orphan Ranch?" Ethan thought of the damage done by the grass fire that had engulfed the ranch just a few months ago, burning most of the buildings to the ground.

Jules nodded. "They did. But only because Lillian insisted there wasn't anything he could do here to help you, and he needed to get back to the ranch."

Ethan agreed with that. Robbie had his hands full cleaning up what was left of the ranch and building back up the part of the herd he'd managed to save. "He's got more than enough of his own problems to deal with."

"That's a fact." Jules took a sip from his own mug of coffee as he continued to study Ethan. "He's worried about you, though. And Ammie." Jules set his mug down and leaned forward. "I've never heard of anyone like this ghost killer that Charles described. A man as big as that who moves without making a sound?" Jules shook his head. "Charles said he and John never even saw him coming at them until it was too late."

"But Christine's father sounded certain that he was no longer with Hawkes," Ethan pointed out.

"You can't be sure of that," Jules argued. "You'll need to be on your guard."

Ethan shrugged. "I always am. But I might have spotted someone at the party that fits the description of the new partner Hawkes is supposed to have acquired."

The marshal sat up straighter. "Who?"

"On the shorter side. Dark hair, dark eyes, solid build." Ethan called up an image of the man in his mind. "Stood on the edge of the group around Ammie."

"Lots of men stand around Ammie," Jules said.

Well aware of that, Ethan shot his friend an annoyed look. "But this one was different. He remained so still I couldn't even tell if he was breathing. And all of his attention was on her." Ethan's jaw hardened at the thought. "Made my skin crawl."

Leaning forward on his elbows, Jules' mouth pulled down at the corners as he listened to Ethan. "I don't like it. Your instincts are good. They've saved my backside on more than one occasion. Did you follow him when he left the party?"

"I couldn't." Ethan rubbed a hand along the side of his

cheek. "I wasn't about to leave Ammie alone or take her with me."

Jules' eyebrows shot up. "Alone? There was a houseful of people there."

"No one I'd trust to keep a proper eye on her."

"Ah." A faint smile crossed the marshal's lips. "Well then, had Ammie ever seen this man before?"

Ethan shrugged. "She said she hadn't, but he wouldn't stand out unless you were looking for him." He shook his head. "And she was busy being the center of every man's attention."

"Every man?" Now Jules did grin. He stroked his chin and made a clucking noise in his throat. "I guess you aren't included among her admirers since she seemed a mite cool toward you this morning. You didn't call her fat again, did you?"

"No." Irritated, Ethan snapped the word out and then clamped his mouth shut. He knew exactly why Ammie was put out with him, and he sure as hell wasn't going to discuss it with Jules.

His friend chuckled. "Don't tell me you came up with a new insult that she's taken issue with?"

"No." Ethan slumped down into his chair. "Let it go, Jules. She'll come around. She always does." At least he hoped that was true since he'd never kissed her before.

"How long do you think you can stay under the same roof with her and not tell her how you feel?"

The bald question had Ethan straightening up and glaring at his friend from beneath lowered brows. "What are you talking about? She's family."

"Not blood, and you know it," Jules said. When Ethan retreated into a stony silence, Jules sighed. "I said the same thing about Dorrie, and thought it was a line that shouldn't be crossed. The thing is, Ethan, in your mind, you crossed that line long ago. Ammie means a lot more to you than just another member of the family. She always has."

Ethan shifted restlessly at the sudden flash of memory of that eight-year-old angel who'd dazzled him so long ago. But he was still that street urchin who'd managed to find a way to be a ranch hand. Ammie lived in a world with friends who occupied mansions on top of Nob Hill. It was where she belonged.

Tamping down feelings that had been simmering far too close to the surface ever since he'd held her in his arms, Ethan fixed a hard stare on his friend. "You're imagining things. Protecting Ammie is a habit. We all protect the women in the family. Once this business with Hawkes is done, I'll be heading out for another stock delivery."

Jules sighed. "If you say so, Ethan. Suit yourself."

Nodding, Ethan stared out the large window at his friend's back. "It suits me fine."

The marshal raised his gaze to the ceiling. "Is that a fact?"

"I THOROUGHLY ENJOYED THE EVENING," Christa declared. She blew a kiss toward Dorrie who was arranging cookies on a plate. "Give that to your mother for me. I looked stunning if I do say so myself. Even Henry complimented my gown, which is nothing short of a small miracle."

Ammie thought her friend did look pleased with the world this morning. Last night her mint-green dress, with a contrasting swathe of cream-colored satin draped across the front of the full skirt, had been particularly becoming, and definitely a creation straight out of Maggie Dolan's shop.

Dorrie's mother was the most sought-after seamstress in the city, and picturing Christa's striking gown reminded Ammie that she had an appointment with Maggie in a few days.

She smiled at Christa. "And did William appreciate your new gown?"

Her friend's laugh spilled through the kitchen. The three women were sitting at the large table that dominated the center of the room. Dorrie's housekeeper had left them to their privacy while she made a trip to the market, and they had just settled in for a cozy talk.

The spacious room, with several windows along the wall and the lingering smell of the morning baking, was always Ammie's first choice to sit in while she visited with her close friend. A practice that had survived her high-society upbringing. Christa had fallen right into the habit without so much as a sound of protest, which, Ammie reflected, was one of the reasons they had become fast friends.

"He most certainly did. And I enjoyed a moonlight stroll with him in the garden." Christa let out a dramatic sigh. "All very proper, of course. William was the perfect gentleman."

"That's not so surprising, Christa. After all, you do have two brothers and a father he'd have to deal with if he didn't behave himself." The teasing note in Dorrie's voice had them all smiling.

"True," Christa agreed. "While I'm sure Henry's idea of defending my honor would be to invent some sort of warning device if a gentleman made any unwanted advances, Adam would have an entirely different approach to the matter."

"I shudder to think about it," Ammie grinned. She could well imagine that simply knowing Adam Fromer was Christa's brother would be enough to keep any man on the straight and narrow path.

"He and Ethan have that in common." Christa took a sip of her tea and plucked a small cookie from the plate. She took a tiny bite and chewed slowly as she turned an amused gaze toward Dorrie. "Has Ethan always followed Ammie around as if there's an invisible rope tying them together?"

Ammie blinked several times and then frowned. "He does not."

Dorrie ignored her and leaned over the table as far as her protruding belly would allow. "Yes. He has," she said in a loud whisper.

When she caught Ammie's glare, Dorrie laughed. "He's always been worse with you than Jules ever was with me, and you've teased me unmercifully about that over the years. So now I can do the same to you. Good heavens, Christa saw it plainly enough after spending only one evening in Ethan's company. Fair is fair." She wrinkled her nose at Ammie's sputtering protest and smiled at Christa. "All Ammie told me was that she left Ethan with you while she went off to talk to Adam. How long did it take before our completely honorary cousin chased after her?"

Christa pursed her lips. "Hmm... I'd say no more than a quarter hour. And it only took that long because I dragged him over to meet Henry."

"And did you ever see him again after he deserted you to find our friend here?"

The blond shook her head. "Not even a glimpse."

Deciding the whole conversation was ridiculous, Ammie audibly sniffed. "Maybe because you were on a moonlight stroll in the garden?"

Christa turned sparkling blue eyes on Ammie. "You can't be so blind that you didn't see the look he gave to Adam when the two of you walked off?"

Dorrie clapped her hands together, her wide smile

showing her absolute delight at that bit of gossip. "How annoyed was he?"

Putting a hand up to her throat, Christa's voice dropped to a whisper. "I was worried there might be fisticuffs in the Lewis' drawing room. And whose side would I take? My brother's, or my best friend's beau?"

"Cousin," Ammie quickly corrected. She pointed a slim finger in Dorrie's direction. "Even she called him our cousin."

"Really?" Christa took another bite of cookie. "Isn't that what Jules called Dorrie before he upped and married her?" Her gaze dropped to the round bulge pressing beneath the front of Dorrie's gown. "I doubt if he thinks of her that way anymore."

Looking at Dorrie, Ammie was sure no one would doubt it. "It isn't the same. I can guarantee that Ethan considers me some sort of distant sister. Or maybe an irritating wart he can't get rid of."

"A wart?" Dorrie laid a hand on her belly. "All right, Amelia Jamison. What happened? You've been put out with Ethan for days now."

"That's right," Christa jumped in. "You certainly were at the party. What did he do?"

"He called her fat the other day," Dorrie said, nodding when Christa gasped. "But he didn't mean it."

Christa turned slightly in her chair, her hand holding her teacup suspended in midair. "Then what *did* he mean?"

Closing her eyes, Ammie bit her lower lip. "He kissed me."

Both women stopped in mid-sentence and gaped at her.

"He what?" Christa's mouth had dropped wide open.

"When?" Dorrie demanded.

"The day the messenger came with the letter about Hawkes," Ammie said. "He found me on the beach."

"And he just walked right up and started kissing you?" Christa's smile reached all the way across her face. "That's very impressive. And romantic."

Ammie rolled her eyes. It might have been if Ethan had left it at that. "No. I was upset about Christine leaving without a word of goodbye, and he kissed me to keep me from crying." She waited for the silence to drag out a bit before finally adding with a sigh. "And then he apologized and called it a mistake."

Christa slapped a palm against her forehead while Dorrie groaned and slumped back in her seat. Feeling exactly the same way, Ammie looked down into her teacup. Her head jerked up when Christa laid a hand on her shoulder.

"The man's a fool." The blond frowned at Dorrie. "You know Ethan best. Why would he do something so foolish?"

"As the kiss or the apology?" Ammie shrugged when both the other women shot her a reproving look.

"Half the men in town would give up their fortunes to be able to kiss you, and propose in the middle of Portsmouth Square the way you've always said you wanted to be proposed to" Christa declared.

Dorrie raised an eyebrow at that. "Only half?"

"Well, some of them are extremely wealthy and old. I'm sure they lost interest in that kind of thing long ago." Christa shrugged when Ammie couldn't hold back a giggle. "I have no idea what the man was thinking when he apologized, but I do know that he had an unusual reaction when I asked him if he was at the party as your cousin, a potential husband, or a prison guard."

What? Ammie stared at her friend. She'd asked Ethan that?

"Which one did he pick?" Dorrie demanded.

"Oh, he didn't." Christa wiggled her eyebrows at Ammie, who was still looking at her in astonishment. "But he only objected to being called a prison guard."

Ammie continued to stir her tea while her two friends carried on with their discussion. They could debate Ethan's reasons for the rest of the day, but she'd already made up her mind that it didn't matter what they were.

He'd been sorry for the kiss, and that was that.

She needed to put it aside and concentrate on the more pressing problem of finding the man who murdered her father. Whether he'd come back to stalk victims in a new hunting ground or to avenge old insults, she was determined to stop him.

And for that, she might need Ethan and his tracking skills. But first, they had to draw the man out. Tapping her finger lightly against the side of her teacup, Ammie considered the possibilities. The Millers, who lived further up Nob Hill, were holding a dance and late-night supper at their mansion in a few days. The invitation had come several weeks ago. If the man Ethan had spotted was indeed Hawkes' new killer, then the Morris' party would be an excellent way to draw him out. All she had to do was let it be known that she would be attending.

Smiling to herself, Ammie lifted her teacup. And she knew the perfect way to go about it.

15

Early the following afternoon, Ethan pulled the carriage to a stop in front of the cheery shop with a bright blue door. He eyed the sign with its white letters proclaiming the establishment as "Kate's Tea Shop".

"What are we doing here?"

Ammie raised an eyebrow. "I've already explained it to you several times, Ethan. We need to be sure it's common knowledge that we'll be attending the Millers' party, and it's the perfect way to do that." She reached over and gave his arm a friendly pat. "It's also a nice place to have a light dinner." When he didn't make a move to exit the carriage, she frowned at him. "You can wait out here if you'd rather. I'll be fine inside."

Resigned, Ethan tied off the reins. "I'm coming with you."

Telling himself it was all part of the plan to flush out Hawkes and his companion, Ethan walked around the carriage so he could help Ammie step to the ground without her tripping over her own skirts. But somewhere inside his head he could hear Robbie's laughter.

He stopped beside the low picket fence and eyed the bank of windows spanning the front of the cozy-looking establishment. It was a far cry from a pot simmering over a fire built under an open sky.

"I guess you come here a lot."

Ammie quirked an eyebrow at him. "With Aunt Lillian ever since I was a little girl. Kate's tea has always been a favorite with us." She smiled. "And a nice change to have a cup without the smell of coffee overpowering the room."

Ethan shifted his weight from one foot to the other. "Tea?"

"A little tea won't kill you, Ethan." She started toward the door with him staring after her.

Not sure if this really was a way to flush out the dark-haired man, or simply Ammie's idea of punishment for the kiss, Ethan slowly followed her up the narrow stone path. When she disappeared inside, he carefully stepped over the threshold, stopping just a foot or two beyond the door as he looked around.

A wall separated the narrow entryway from the open room on the other side. He listened for a moment to the gentle flow of soft conversations. Judging by the generally higher pitch, he was definitely headed into purely female territory.

Exactly as Robbie had warned him.

There was a row of hooks inside the door, and he was relieved to see a couple of hats hanging on them. At least he wouldn't be the only man in the place. As he removed his own and placed it on the nearest hook, he took in an appreciable sniff of the air. The shop smelled heavenly with its mixed aromas of freshly baked bread and a spice he didn't recognize, but had his mouth watering.

Looking forward to a little dinner while Ammie did

whatever needed to be done to start the gossips talking about the Millers' party, he walked over to where she was waiting for him.

"Place smells nice."

"Thank you." The booming, cheery voice had Ethan looking over Ammie's head. He hadn't noticed the woman in the snow-white apron standing a few feet away. Her blue eyes lit with amusement, she aimed a wide smile at him. "Welcome to my shop, Ethan. I was beginning to think I'd never get a look at you."

With no ready response to that, Ethan settled for a nod. The noise level had dropped considerably, and when he took a quick glance around, Ethan had a good idea why.

Kate's voice had easily carried through the cozy space, and he was now the center of attention for most of the women sitting at the small tables scattered across the gleaming wooden floor. The heat crept up the back of his neck as Ammie curled a hand around his arm, just above his elbow.

"I didn't think Ethan would need an introduction." She raised her voice slightly as she smiled at Kate. "I've been telling him it's past time he met my friends and was introduced to society. He's in town to escort me to the Millers' reception."

Kate gave Ammie a conspiratorial grin as she led them to a table on the far side of the shop while Ethan trailed along, wondering what was wrong with the few empty tables they'd passed by. "Wonderful. I understand it's going to be quite the glittering affair."

As Ethan dutifully pulled out Ammie's chair and waited while she got settled, he glanced out the window. Their table was placed right next to one, and several women strolling by on the sidewalk slowed their pace as they stared at the couple framed by the glass.

Feeling like he was on display for the entire city to stare at, Ethan stepped around Kate to pull out his own chair. He eyed it for a long moment, not at all sure the daintily curved seat and spindly legs would hold his weight. If he ended up on his backside in the middle of the teashop, he'd not only never hear the end of it from Jules, Robbie, or Ammie, he'd also have to pay for the privilege of breaking one of Kate's chairs.

Hoping for the best, Ethan gingerly sat on the delicate seat and held his breath as it creaked beneath his weight. But much to his relieved surprise, the thing didn't splinter into pieces. He'd never be able to relax in it, but at least he wasn't sitting on the floor. He caught the look of a man perched on the edge of his own chair a few tables away. He gave a resigned smile as he nodded at Ethan.

"I'm sure you're having a new gown made for the occasion?"

Kate's voice penetrated Ethan's dark thoughts about wobbly chairs. A new gown? He'd bet everything he owned, including Brat, that Ammie already had a closet full of them.

"Of course. I have an appointment tomorrow at Maggie's for the final fitting."

Ethan's gaze snapped over to Ammie. She smiled at Kate while he fixed a hard stare on her innocent expression. Dress shop?

He'd been to Maggie's a few times when he'd been growing up, and once not too long ago with Jules when the marshal had been chasing after Dorrie. That should have been enough for any man in one lifetime. Since he wasn't going to let Ammie out of his sight whenever they were not in the house, and he had no intention of lurking about a dress shop, then she wasn't going either.

Firm in that decision, Ethan looked up when Kate said his name.

"Good heavens, Ethan Mayes. Where were you? I've already asked you three times if you'd like sweetener with your tea."

"He doesn't, Kate. He gets a bit distracted when he's hungry." Ammie shook her head to Kate's amused smile.

The shop owner winked at her. "You seem to know your cousin very well."

"We grew up together," Ammie said before Ethan managed to get his mouth open. "Aunt Lillian tried to make tea drinkers out of all the boys, but didn't have any success, I'm afraid."

Nodding her understanding, Kate studied Ethan for a moment. "I'm not surprised. Even Cook prefers coffee, and Dina once told me that he'd grown up in England."

She ran her hands along the sides of her apron. "Well, let me get something for your cousin to eat, then maybe he'll be able to talk a bit more." She gave Ethan's shoulder a motherly pat before bustling off.

"Ethan, where are your manners?" Ammie leaned forward and lowered her voice.

Feeling genuinely bad that he'd been rude to the affable Kate, Ethan blew out a breath and ran a distracted hand across his cheek. "I'm sorry. I'm not used to being in a place like this."

Ammie looked around before returning a wide-eyed gaze to Ethan. "Like this?" She frowned slightly. "What's so unusual about this place?"

He shrugged. "It's not too sturdy."

"Sturdy?" Ammie's frown turned down even more. "You

think Kate's is where frivolous people go when they have nothing better to do?"

He matched her frown with one of his own. He was not taking a stroll with her down that path again. "No. I mean the table's barely big enough for a teapot, and I'm not sure how much longer this chair is going to hold me up."

"Hold you...?" Ammie blinked and then let out a rare giggle.

It was such a feminine sound, and so fit the way she looked in her soft lilac dress with a matching ribbon weaving through the rich brown of her hair, that Ethan smiled and then laughed, unmindful of the attention it drew from the people around them. "I'm glad you find me sprawled out on the floor so funny."

"I'm not amused," Ammie choked out, raising a hand to cover her smile as she shook her head in denial. "Really, I'm not. I simply hadn't thought about..."

When she trailed off, Ethan grinned at her. "The difference in our sizes?" He held up a hand, palm out. "Which is considerably larger than yours."

Ammie inclined her head while her eyes gleamed with held-back laughter. "Why, thank you."

Kate suddenly appeared, holding a tray with a teapot and two cups and saucers. She deftly balanced it against her hip as she set the items on the table. Once everything was in its place, she stepped back. Her bright smile dimmed a bit when she looked at Ethan.

"You really don't like tea?"

"He loves it. He simply won't admit it to the rest of the men in the family."

Still aware of his earlier lack of manners with Kate, Ethan quickly nodded his head at Ammie's small lie, and was rewarded when Kate's smile regained its friendly shine.

She leaned closer and whispered. "It will be our secret. Cross my heart." She nodded her assurance before straightening up. After promising to bring the rest of their refreshments out shortly, she left them alone.

Ethan watched silently as Ammie put half a teaspoon of sugar in her tea and stirred it while she stared out the window. She seemed relaxed, and as much as he enjoyed just looking at her, there was something they needed to discuss.

"Ammie," he began, waiting until her gaze shifted over to him. "We need to talk about what we should do from here on."

She leaned back in her seat and stared at him. "What do you mean?"

"We need to be honest with each other."

"Honest?" she repeated before drawing in an audible breath. "I'm not going to be throwing myself at you, if that's what you're worried about, Ethan."

He frowned. "Not throwing yourself, but we need to stay close, it's the best way."

Her mouth dropped open and then snapped shut again when her foot started tapping against the wooden floor. Wondering what he'd said to get her back up this time, Ethan tried again.

"I can't keep you safe if I'm not with you."

"Oh." Ammie sounded confused, but it was so fleeting that Ethan thought he'd imagined it when she lifted her teacup. "We *are* spending all our time together."

"Almost," Ethan admitted. "But while you were seeing callers this morning, I went out to check on the stables Luke has here in town."

"I know. Helen told me."

Ethan wasn't sure how he felt about having all his movements reported to Ammie, but as long as he was staying in a house full of women, he doubted there was much he could do about it.

"How was Henry?"

Now thoroughly exasperated, Ethan's gaze narrowed. "How did you know I met Henry there?"

"Christa mentioned it in a note she sent around. We're going to meet at Aunt Maggie's dress shop tomorrow."

Thinking the telegraph office could learn a thing or two from these women, Ethan shook his head. "Henry's fine. He thinks we should change our feed and put in a system of ropes and pulleys to bring water into the stable."

"Does he?" Ammie laughed. "Henry is always inventing something or other. He has a whole collection of crushed rocks in different colors in that shed he works in behind his parents' home."

"It wouldn't surprise me. I liked him," Ethan admitted. "Don't know why. He's too absent-minded to work with animals much. And has a habit of not paying attention to what's going on around him. He almost got kicked by my horse. Brat didn't appreciate how close Henry was standing to her hind legs."

"Your horse is a mare and you named her Brat?"

Seeing another one of those black pits opening up in front of him, Ethan concentrated on sounding as if there was nothing unusual about that. "The horse tends to act up a lot." When Ammie's eyes narrowed, he quickly moved on. "Since I don't have a Christa to keep me informed of your whereabouts, I'd appreciate it if you'd save me some time from having to track you down and just tell me what your plans are."

He braced himself for an argument but relaxed again when Ammie nodded.

"I will if you will."

He grinned at her. "That's a bargain I can make." He hesitated a moment before continuing on. "I have to go out for a while tonight. There's someone I need to meet."

"About Papa's murder? Because I want to..."

He stopped her protest by reaching over and covering one of her hands with his. "He's an old friend, Ammie. I haven't seen him in a while. I wanted you to know, and I'd like your word that you'll stay inside while I'm gone."

"Oh." She waited as if she expected him to say something more. But when he remained silent, she audibly sighed as she picked up her spoon and stirred her tea. "All right. You have my word." When he continued to stare at her, she tilted her head to the side. "Is there something else?"

Ethan shrugged. "Nope. That's my only plan besides following you around." When she smiled, he did too. "Care to tell me where we'll be going beside the Millers' get-together?"

"I've already mentioned about visiting Aunt Maggie's shop."

Not likely, Ethan thought, but would leave that argument until tomorrow.

"And as you said, the Millers' ball, and then I'll need to see to a few things the following night for a new client."

He sat up straighter. "What kind of things?"

"You're welcome to come along, if you'd like. Your tracking skills might come in handy, although this isn't exactly open country."

Ammie's roundabout answer wasn't what he'd been looking for, but he'd take it. As long as he could keep an eye on her, he was willing to help her with her society friends.

He'd barely nodded before Kate appeared with another

tray. This one had two plates, each with a single biscuit and several thin slices of ham next to it. Once she had them placed on the table to her satisfaction, Kate set a small crock of butter in front of the couple with a flourish.

"There you are. Enjoy your meal."

Meal? Ethan looked at the plate that was barely bigger than his fist, and still had plenty of room for the single biscuit and two pieces of meat.

"Thank you, Kate. It looks delicious."

He shot Ammie an incredulous look, but managed to mumble a thanks before Kate sauntered away.

His brows beetled together as Ammie cut off a small piece of ham. Determined to be polite, Ethan stabbed at the meat with his fork and lifted the entire slice up. It was so thin he would have sworn he could see right through it.

Ammie pointed her own fork at him. "I know you like ham, Ethan."

"When I get some," he muttered to himself. When she gave him a questioning look, he managed a smile. "I was just taking a moment to admire it."

Her lips quirked upward, but she didn't say anything as she broke her biscuit in half and reached for the butter crock.

An hour later, Ethan gratefully followed Ammie out of the stable behind her house and into the back door leading to the kitchen. The room was empty, and Ethan gave a longing look toward the stove. It wouldn't take much to poke the banked fire to life and heat up a strong cup of coffee. It might help the growling in his stomach.

"Sit down, Ethan." Ammie pointed at the large table in the center of the room as she lifted an apron off the hook near the door.

He stared, wondering what she was doing. "What?"

She rolled her eyes as she walked over to the pantry shelves that lined the back wall and removed a basket filled with eggs. Heading back toward the stove, Ammie set the basket onto the long counter next to it and reached for a heavy skillet.

Ethan pulled out one of the chairs tucked under the table and turned it around. Straddling it, he sat down and rested his arms along the back. "What are you doing?"

"Making you fried eggs." She looked over one shoulder and wrinkled her nose. "I could hear your stomach grumbling during the entire ride home."

He was dumbfounded. "You can cook?"

When she'd finished stirring the embers and closing the stove's door, Ammie turned and faced him. "Why do you sound so surprised? Of course I can. The best cook in the city helped raise me." She straightened the frying pan on top of the stove and placed a spoonful of bacon grease from a jar nearby into the pan. As it was heating up, she went back to the pantry shelves for a loaf of bread that was covered with a checkered cloth.

"I've also spent nights on the trail traveling to The Orphan Ranch, and on the beach with the aunts." She turned around, a fork in her hand, and smiled. "Although whenever the aunts wanted to stay on the beach, the uncles would make a big show of waving goodbye, and then follow us. They spent the night in the trees." She laughed softly. "Every one of them thought that we didn't know they were there."

Ethan shifted in his chair. "Watching over our women isn't an easy habit to ignore."

"Oh, we're all well aware of that, Ethan."

A comfortable silence fell over the kitchen as he watched Ammie efficiently slice thick pieces of bread and place them on the plate. She hollowed out a space in the center of each slice and slid a fried egg into it. It wasn't long before his mouth was watering.

When he looked up at her, she put her hands on her hips and tilted her head to the side. "As you see, I can cook. Do you have any other questions?"

Ethan stood up and turned his chair back around before plucking a fork from a jar in the center of the table. He sat down and looked over when she set a mug of coffee next to his plate and took a seat across from him. All she had in front of her was a cup of tea.

"One question." He picked up his fork and cut into his meal. "What do you need another dress for?"

"Oh. Just because it seemed like a good idea." She raised an eyebrow at him. "Why did you name your mare 'Brat'?"

Ethan ducked his head and concentrated on his food.

16

Ethan moved silently through the streets. He'd left Ammie's house just after nightfall and headed for The Crimson Rose. After telling Charles about the man he'd spotted at the Lewis' party, he went upstairs to the room always kept ready for him and traded his hat and boots for a pair of shoes with softer leather soles, and a dark knit cap pulled down low over his forehead. It had been almost midnight before he'd started to make his way across the Barbary Coast.

It was another hour before he spotted the big man, moving through the shadows along a deserted block of buildings near the black waters of the bay. It looked like his old friend still haunted the same section of the city that he had almost twenty years before.

Keeping behind his quarry, and careful to stay out of his sight, Ethan slowly worked his way closer until he could reach over and jam a closed fist into the unsuspecting man's back.

"I've got a shotgun."

"You've got a hand on my back." The big man whirled

around and slapped a meaty palm on top of Ethan's shoulder.

"You've gotten better at sneakin' up on a man."

Ethan grinned, his teeth showing white in the darkness. "I've had a lot of opportunity to practice."

Slab nodded his shaggy head. "I've heard."

Taking a step back, Ethan stuck his hands into the pockets of his jacket as he looked around. "Doesn't seem to have changed much."

"Grown some. Gotten more dangerous." Slab turned so the building was at his back. "What are you doin' out here?"

"Looking for you."

The big man grinned and held up two large hands in surrender. "I'm sorry about that dunkin' in the water. Miss Ammie asked me to keep you from followin' her." He leaned down slightly and squinted at Ethan through the darkness. "Why were you searchin' for her?"

His old friend shrugged. "What makes you think I was looking for her?"

"You called out to her, Cracker. I heard it clear enough. That's why I pushed you into that horse trough."

Drawing in a deep breath at the name he'd walked away from long ago, Ethan stared down at the end of the street, watching the fog slowly creep along, engulfing everything in its path. "I'm here to keep an eye on her.

"Have anything to do with that Haunt what killed her pa?" Slab lowered his voice as he looked around. "I ain't never known what happened to that man, if'n he was a man."

Ethan let out a soft whistle. "Is that who murdered Eli Jamison? The Haunt?" He remembered the whispered stories from the time he'd lived in the deserted buildings and back alleyways. The Haunt was said to have appeared from nowhere, and killed without his victims ever laying eyes on him.

Ethan's brow furrowed as he turned the old stories over in his mind. They most likely did spring from the man who'd traveled with Simeon Hawkes and murdered Ammie's father. But the Haunt had supposedly killed many men. Even accounting for the legend growing over the years, it was just as Master Kwan had said. Eli Jamison wasn't Charles' ghost killer's only victim.

"And no one knows where the Haunt is now?" Ethan asked, using Slab's term for Hawkes assassin.

Slab shook his head. "No. And you'd best not say his name too loud, or you might call him back."

Ethan doubted that. It was more likely that the man was dead himself. And probably not from natural causes. "Have there been any other killings lately?"

Slab raised a thick hand and stroked it down his beard. "There's always killings goin' on in the Coast, Cracker. And in them opium dens too. But I ain't heard of any like the Haunt used to do."

"Not beaten, Slab. With a knife that had a very thin blade."

"Could be," Slab said slowly. His hand did one last pass down the length of his beard before he shoved it into the pocket of the heavy coat with the tattered sleeves that he was wearing. "One slice across the neck. Cut was deep but not as wide as a regular knife."

"Who?" Ethan asked.

Slab hunched his shoulders against the cold the fog had brought. The two men were now surrounded by the gray mist as it continued its slow journey down the street. "Two that I know of. One was a gent and the other a miner who'd had a bit of luck at the tables."

Making a mental note to ask Jules about the dead "gent", as Slab had called him, Ethan took another quick look up and down the narrow passageway of mud that passed for a street in the Barbary Coast section of the city. "Did anyone see these men get their throats cut?"

The big man frowned. "You gonna tell that friend of yours who wears a badge?"

Ethan shook his head. "No. I just want to talk to anyone who saw the murder. I only need a description."

"What's this got to do with Miss Ammie?"

"He might be traveling with the same man who hired the Haunt to kill for him all those years ago." Ethan paused. "And that would include Miss Ammie's father."

Slab stood up a little straighter before leaning over to get a closer look at his old friend's face. "You think he might want to do to Miss Ammie what he done to her pa?"

A question that had plagued Ethan ever since Helen had burst into Charles' study at The Crimson Rose. "I won't let that happen."

With a grunt of approval, Slab jerked his head to the side. "Will that fancy life of yours let you buy a man a beer?"

"It would," Ethan nodded. "You have a place in mind?"

"Where old Ollie sits at night. He don't talk with many people, but he does with me." Slab's big shoulders moved up and down. "I bring him food when I can."

"And why do we want to have a beer with old Ollie?" Ethan asked as he fell into step, lengthening his stride so he could keep up with Slab.

"It's Ollie who saw that miner git his throat slit from one ear to the other."

They walked along in silence for half a block. "I sure don't want Miss Ammie to be bothered none, "Slab finally said. "You need help lookin' for this man?"

Ethan considered it before slowly nodding. "It would be good to have a few men who can find their way easily around the city." He looked around. "It's changed since I lived here."

Slab laughed. The sound echoed down the street and bounced off several walls. "You knew all the hidey-holes, Cracker. You saved Shannon from some bad men that night she got herself trapped."

"Luke saved her," Ethan corrected.

"He couldn't have done it without you." Slab turned a corner and kept walking down a block that had more life and noise than the one they'd just left. "Isn't that why he took you out to live on that ranch of his?"

"Most likely." Ethan's gaze went over every face they passed, looking for anyone who might mean trouble.

"Are most of our old acquaintances still around?" Ethan asked, making conversation as he kept up his study of the people and buildings they went by.

Slab chuckled. "Rabbit got hisself a new callin'. He's taken up preachin' at a church on one of them streets off of Market." He grinned when Ethan laughed. "And Bella got married to a miner and left to find their fortune in silver." Slab sighed. "Haven't seen her since."

Deep furrows appeared over the big man's bushy eyebrows. "Got a good man who could help us with the search. He knows all the places a man might hide. That's why he's called Mouse."

"Ammie mentioned him, along with Wang Wei."

"Can't use Wang Wei. He's busy doin' somethin' for his grandpa so I haven't seen him much lately." Slab stopped suddenly and pulled Ethan deeper into the shadow of the wall running alongside the wooden walkway. "I heard your pa came lookin' fer you a few years back."

Surprised by the question, Ethan tilted his head and frowned up at Slab. "He did. But I was grown by the time he got around to it."

"Did he find you out on that ranch?"

"He didn't have to, Slab. I found out he was asking around so I tracked him here in town. I made it clear he wasn't welcome at the ranch."

Slab was back to stroking his beard. "Word is that he got hisself killed in a bar fight."

Ethan crossed his arms over his chest. He didn't know where Slab was going with this. "I heard the same."

The big man hung his head and shuffled his feet for a moment, looking so sheepish that Ethan smiled.

"What's wrong, Slab?"

"I fergot until after I told you about Mouse."

Holding onto his patience, Ethan waited while Slab rubbed his chin. It was a sure sign he was thinking something over.

Finally dropping his hand and taking in a deep breath, Slab shot Ethan a sideways look. "Yer pa was punching a man much smaller than him. Bloodied him up pretty good before Mouse stepped in."

Ethan's eyebrows shot up. He wasn't surprised his father had beaten the daylights out of someone much smaller. The truth was, it sounded like him. But Ethan had never known who had killed his father. Of course, he'd never asked either.

"It were a kind of accident," Slab rushed on. "Mouse only pushed him to git him off the little guy. Yer father hit his head against that brick wall. Mouse thought he was jist knocked out cold, so he left him there. Didn't figure out he was dead until the next morning when yer pa was still lyin' right where he fell."

When Ethan didn't say anything, Slab rolled up on the balls of his feet and then back down again. "I'm sorry, Cracker. I won't ask for Mouse's help if'n you don't want me to."

Since he'd had no feelings for his pa long before the man had taken off for the gold fields, leaving his nine-year-old son to fend for himself in the city, Ethan only shrugged. "Sounds like an accident. I don't have any problems working with Mouse." He glanced down the street. "How much further until we reach the place where old Ollie sits every night?"

"A couple of blocks." Slab pointed a finger down the street. "We turn again at that corner down there."

"Let's move then." Ethan started walking. It only took Slab two strides to fall into step with him again. Flipping the collar of his coat up against the chill of the night, Ethan looked over at Slab. "Before we get there, maybe you can tell me something about what you, Mouse and Wang Wei do for Miss Ammie." He shoved his hands into his coat pockets. "And have you ever had a meal at a tea shop?"

17

"INTERESTING PLACE TO SPEND YOUR MORNING."

Ethan glared at Jules as the marshal took a long, slow look around Maggie's crowded dress shop. "Must be, since you're here too."

Jules' amused gaze returned to Ethan. "I've already explained that I love my wife and make it a habit of keeping her happy." He lifted an eyebrow. "Why are you here?"

Sure that several of the women standing close to them were avidly listening in on their conversation, Ethan hunched his shoulders over and lowered his voice. "Ammie needs a new gown for the party."

"Is that a fact?" Jules' grin remained firmly in place. "Ammie's had Maggie make her a closet full of gowns, and I don't recall ever seeing you in here with her before."

The tracker gritted his teeth. It was obvious Jules was having a good deal of fun at his expense. "You're the one who said I had to come back to town to protect Ammie and Aunt Charlotte. Well, that's what I'm doing."

"Seeing some danger in all these feathers and bolts of cloth?" Jules chuckled when Ethan's shoulders sunk in even more, then held up his hands in surrender when his friend took a deliberate step closer. "I'm done. But since you're here, I'll leave Dorrie in your hands."

"Mine?" Ethan's head whipped around. He spotted Dorrie, the long ends of a fringed shawl draping over her extended belly, chatting with Maggie at the far end of the counter. "She's *your* wife."

"And I escorted her here like a good husband. But I have someone I need to meet, so I'm leaving it to you to keep an eye on her." Jules nodded.

He started to turn away when Ethan shot out a hand and grabbed onto his arm. "Wait just a minute. I can't watch a... a..." He stumbled to a stop, not sure how to get out what he was trying to say.

"A woman carrying a child?" Jules supplied helpfully, making Ethan's face go even redder. "It's not hard, Ethan. If something happens, get her to Dr. Abby." He narrowed his eyes. "And be sure you send someone by the house to fetch me."

Ethan froze to the spot. I something happens? What the hell did he mean by that? Feeling as if he was lost in a dense fog, he moved his head in a hard shake. "Do what?"

"Dr. Abby," Jules repeated patiently, the amusement back in his eyes. "Cade's wife. My sister-in-law who's also a doctor. Remember her?"

"Dorrie is *your* wife."

"We've already established that."

Ethan ran an agitated hand across his cheek. "You're the one who should be taking her to the doctor, not me."

"Last I heard, you still know how to handle a horse and drive a carriage." Jules pried off Ethan's hand and took a step toward the door. "I'll leave ours here in case you need it."

"What?" By the time Ethan got his horrified reaction

under control, Jules was gone. Ammie had disappeared behind a dark green curtain leading into the back of the shop almost as soon as they'd stepped inside. He stared at the flimsy barrier for a solid minute, hoping she'd reappear and take Dorrie into the back with her.

"Ethan Mayes. You come here and give me a proper hello."

Maggie's demand had Ethan reluctantly turning in her direction. He carefully walked to the end of the counter, sidestepping several other customers and doing his best not to knock over or break anything along the way. He felt like he towered over everything and everyone in the shop. Maggie watched his slow progress, her moss-green eyes crinkled at the corners and her mouth turned up into a smile.

"Now don't you make the very picture of a man not knowin' where he's at." The soft lilt of Ireland still wove its way through Maggie Dolan's voice. "I'm surprised to see you in me shop."

"Ammie needed to come," Ethan mumbled. He ducked his head at Dorrie, then gave her a wary look.

Maggie's eyebrows rose up a notch or two. "You're here for Ammie is it?" She glanced over at the green curtain. "Lillian told me that her mam appeared on her doorstep, talkin' about the man who killed Ammie's da." Maggie looked back at Ethan. "And then you showed up to be sure our Ammie stays safe."

"That's right."

"You're a fine man, Ethan, to be lookin' after her that way." Maggie nodded her approval. "But I'm wonderin' if you're intendin' to be standin' about me shop for her entire fittin'?"

Ethan frowned, wondering how long a dress fitting took. "I need to keep an eye on her."

"Which you can be doin' from the carriage in front of the shop." Maggie straightened to her full height, which was about to the top of Ethan's shoulder, and crossed her arms. "Your frown is scarin' away me customers."

He didn't doubt that. He'd already seen several of the women make a hasty exit. But he couldn't do much about it. As long as Ammie was here, he would be too.

"I hope he isn't going to hang about inside," Dorrie said. She leaned over the counter and dropped her voice to a loud whisper. "He's giving me the same eye that Jules does. As if he expects me to give birth right where I'm standing."

Horrified, Ethan's gaze automatically dropped to Dorrie's belly before it snapped back up to her face. "Don't."

"Don't?" Dorrie laughed. "Don't what?"

"Just don't," Ethan repeated a bit more fiercely. He mentally made a plan to strangle his best friend when he saw him again.

"Men have weak stomachs when it comes to birthin'," Maggie said with a casual shrug. "I thought your da would end up cold on the floor before your sister made her appearance." She pursed her lips and studied her daughter. "You're carryin' the wee one high. I'm thinkin' you'll be givin' me a granddaughter to love."

Dorrie ran a gentle hand over the mound in front of her. "I don't know, Mam. Jules said he'd be happy with either a son or a daughter." She smiled softly. "I will be too."

Closing his eyes, Ethan willed himself to be somewhere else. Anywhere else but standing in a dress shop listening to talk of babies.

"There are also a few things we should start thinkin'

about that you'll need during the birthin. I knew you'd be comin' today, so I asked Doctor Abby for a list."

When Maggie reached into the pocket of the apron covering her blouse and skirt, Ethan did a quick about-face. No friendship was worth him listening to the women discuss the details of bringing a child into the world. Deciding that the seamstress was right and he could keep an eye on Ammie from the seat of the carriage out front, Ethan made a quick bolt for the door.

He was almost there when a sturdily built matron suddenly stepped into his path, forcing him to do a quick change of direction to the side — and into a tall hat rack with a half dozen creations on display. He made a quick grab for the rack to keep it from being knocked clear to the ground as ribbons, flowers, and feathers went flying through the air.

The matron's scream was still ringing in his ears as he stood with his arms around the wooden rack, listening to the sound of footsteps marching down the narrow aisle.

"Stop crushing me hats, Ethan." Maggie gave him a sharp poke in the shoulder.

"Yes, ma'am," Ethan mumbled as he carefully straightened out, setting the rack upright before taking a step back. Something crunched under his foot. He looked down at the woven hat with several wide ribbons that he'd smashed under his boot. With his whole face and the back of his neck on fire, he raised his eyes until he met Maggie's annoyed gaze.

Ethan opened his mouth to apologize, but not one sound came out.

"Raise that big boot of yours, Ethan Mayes, and get it off of me hat."

Hastily obeying, Ethan lifted his foot and balanced on

one leg as he took a quick look over his shoulder before he stepped back. He wanted to be sure there wasn't anything else behind him to knock over.

Maggie bent at the waist and lifted the jumbled mess of ribbons and straw to eye level, turning it carefully around as she examined it. "Didn't you have somewhere you were goin', Ethan?"

"I'm sorry, Maggie," he finally managed to get out, nodding when she only pointed a finger at the door.

Two seconds later he was outside, taking a calming breath. He'd barely closed the door when he heard what sounded like the entire shop burst into laughter. Sincerely wishing he'd been quicker out the door that morning than Jules had been, Ethan stomped to the carriage and spent a pleasant ten minutes conjuring up all sorts of ways he'd have his revenge on the marshal.

"Looks like you've got a lot on your mind."

Ethan closed his eyes and wondered if the day could get any worse. He turned his head and glared at the tall man with the piercing blue eyes who was standing next to the carriage. Adam Fromer smiled back at him.

The man looked perfect in his light-colored trousers and jacket. Ethan thought he must not favor hats since he wasn't wearing one, and couldn't help but notice the high glossy shine on Adam's black boots, which were very different from the well-worn and dusty leather ones that he always wore.

"Fromer. You're out early."

Adam raised an eyebrow and took a gold pocket watch out of his vest. "A perfectly respectable hour for a gentleman to be about." He snapped the lid of the watch closed and replaced it into his vest pocket before he glanced over his shoulder toward the front of the shop. "I take it you've been banished from Maggie's establishment?"

Resenting the statement, even if it was true, Ethan propped a boot on top of the foot board and shrugged. "What makes you think that?"

"Not hard to figure out. Ammie's inside and you're out here sitting in her carriage." Adam grinned. "You don't usually get this far away from her."

Ethan frowned. "Her carriage? You seem to know a lot about Ammie."

"So do you."

"I grew up with her."

"Ah, yes. The claim of a family connection. Cousin of some sort, I believe." At Ethan's silent stare, Adam shrugged. "I've been her business associate for several years."

For years? Ethan's jaw hardened. No wonder the two of them acted as if they knew each other pretty well. He also wondered why Adam Fromer had never been mentioned to him before. Something else for him to discuss with Jules. "That's a long time."

"Not for me. I tend to keep my business associates for much longer than that." He stepped forward and leaned an arm against the carriage wheel. "Since we're exchanging our histories with Amelia Jamison, how long have you been in love with her?"

The trackers boot hit the floor of the carriage with a loud thud. "Don't rich men have anything to do but stroll down the streets?"

"We do," Adam said. "We also know when it's prudent to steer a conversation in another direction. I've made a few inquiries about our friend, Mr. Hawkes."

Ethan tamped down his immediate objection to Adam Fromer becoming involved in the search for Hawkes, which only meant that Ethan would have to spend more time in his company. But at this point, any information would be welcome, no matter who was the source, so he kept his gaze on the tall man standing next to the carriage and waited.

"No one seems to have heard of the man, or can recall anyone with his description."

"So, nothing," Ethan grunted.

"Something," Adam corrected. "There isn't even a sliver of a rumor about the man. Not at the rail station or any of the hotels. He might be staying in a leased house, but there aren't many of those in the better areas of town, and I've looked into them as well. My contacts have told me that Charles has also sent word out across the city, and still no one has anything to tell either of us. It's as if this Hawkes doesn't even exist."

Remaining silent, Ethan thought that over for a moment. If a man wanted to be invisible, it could be done in a city the size of San Francisco. Cracker had certainly been able to do it.

"Hawkes knows he's being hunted."

Adam crossed his arms over his chest and gazed down the street. "It would seem so. Either that, or he's avoiding repeating a mistake he'd made the last time he was in San Francisco."

"What about the man at the Lewis's party?" Ethan asked.

"Burgess." Adam straightened away from the wheel and turned to face Ethan. "Short, dark hair and eyes, solid build. Got the impression that he didn't need any padding in the shoulders of that coat he was wearing."

A name was better than nothing, but it still didn't tell Ethan much. "Have you heard about him approaching anyone to invest in something?"

The society gentleman shook his head. "He has money of his own, apparently. And the story of where he came from is strangely muddled. Some said New York, others Philadelphia. But he doesn't seem to lack for funds."

Ethan wondered if this Burgess had gotten his wealth from hapless gents who'd wandered too far into the Barbary Coast, or from miners who'd had a good night at a gaming table. He matched the description Ethan had heard from old Ollie the night before. But if that were true, he'd need to replenish his funds on a regular basis.

"I still think he could lead us to Hawkes." Ethan ran a hand down his cheek. "He's the one. I can feel it."

"Agreed," Adam said. "We'll both keep a close watch at the Millers' reception tomorrow night." He smiled as he glanced back at Maggie's shop. "Which I assume is why Ammie has you sitting in front of the dress shop."

Relenting a little, Ethan grunted. "She had a fitting."

"The last time I accompanied Christa into the shop, I bumped into Maggie's assistant who was carrying a basket full of buttons."

Grinning at the thought, Ethan leaned back against the carriage seat and once again propped his boot up. "What happened?"

Adam shrugged. "What you'd expect. Buttons went flying everywhere, and Maggie banned me from the shop." He joined in with Ethan's laughter. "So, what did *you* do?"

"Knocked over a rack of hats and then stepped on one."

Eying Ethan's large boot with mud cased along its edges, Adam nodded. "That will definitely get you sent out to the carriage."

18

AMMIE PLACED HER HAND INTO ETHAN'S AND STEPPED OUT OF the carriage. The blue satin of her gown shimmered in the moonlight as it flowed around her with any movement she made. But the magic of the night was lost when Ethan let go of her hand as soon as her feet were on the ground. She peeked up at him through her lashes, wondering how long he intended to be in a sour mood over a crushed hat.

Because he'd been in one ever since they'd returned from Maggie's shop.

As they walked side by side up the wide stone path leading to the Millers' mansion, Ammie came to a dead stop and glared at her escort and supposed chaperon for the evening. "Why are you squirming around like that, Ethan?"

He stuck a finger into the stiff collar at his neck and made a face. "It's too tight."

She brushed his hand aside and reached up to straighten out his neckcloth. "Lillian told me she'd picked out these clothes herself, and had you put them on and show her before you left her home. She said everything fit perfectly." Ammie ran a hand lightly down the front of his formal coat. "You look very handsome."

Ethan stuck out his chin. "It's too tight."

"Fine." Ammie threw up her hands and continued up the walk as Ethan stomped along beside her. When they'd reached the top of the wide stone steps leading to the impressive front porch, she stopped again to face him. "You're acting like a child, Ethan Mayes. If you don't want to attend this party, then feel free to take the carriage and go home. I'm sure Adam can keep an eye on me in case this Mr. Burgess makes an appearance."

"He'll be here, and I'm staying."

Ammie shrugged at that. "Fine. But no one is going to come near me with that scowl on your face, so do your watching from a distance." Not waiting to hear his response to that, Ammie stepped into the line of people making their way toward the front door.

Once inside, she relinquished her intricate, black lace shawl to a maid, and wandered into the large reception room to the right of the entryway. Wide chandeliers with candles mounted over crystal droplets marched down the center of the ceiling, throwing off light and shadows, and glistening off the gold and diamonds adorning the necks and hands of the crowd of people below. The brilliant colors of the women's gowns shone against the black backdrop of the men's attire, and at the far end of the room, the orchestra had begun to test their instruments.

Taking up a spot just inside the door, Ammie took a moment to get her bearings while a silent Ethan stood next to her. She glanced around, trying to spot a friend among the ever-shifting sea of people wandering throughout the room.

On the opposite side, several large doors were open to a

wide balcony, and in the distance was the breathtaking view of the bay, half of it sparkling in the moonlight and the other half shrouded in a creeping bank of fog. Ammie smiled when she saw Christa artfully posed next to the dark-brown curtains, making her lavender dress and blond curls all the more striking.

"What's so funny?"

Turning her face to smile at Ethan, Ammie inclined her head in the direction of the balcony. "I was admiring Christa's excellent eye for the dramatic."

Ethan looked over toward the open doors. "Whose attention is she trying to get?"

"With that frown, clearly not yours," Ammie sniffed. When Ethan only shrugged, she let out an exasperated sigh.

"William Milton, would be my guess," Ethan said.

Surprised, Ammie's brow furrowed. "How did you know that?"

"They seemed to enjoy each other's company at the last party we attended."

Ammie's eyes narrowed slightly as she glanced back at Christa. "Did they?" She shifted her gaze to Ethan. "You should ask her to dance." When he shook his head, she prodded her elbow into his side. "I know you can dance, Ethan, and it will be expected of you. Isn't there anyone here you'd like to partner with?" When he only grunted, she shook her head. "Am I supposed to know what that means?"

"No."

She waited, but it didn't take long for her to realize that was all he was going to say. "No, what?"

"I'm not dancing."

Wondering how in the world he expected them to catch anyone if he simply skulked about, Ammie smiled and nodded at a passing couple. "All right. But I *do* intend to dance."

For the first time since they'd left the house, Ethan looked directly at her and frowned. "With who?"

Ammie rolled her eyes. "I don't know. I'll have to wait and see who asks me." She tilted her head and gave him a pasted-on smile. "In the meantime, I need to go and talk to Christa."

Picking up her skirts, she threaded her way across the room, not caring if Ethan had followed her or not. She was tired of trying to decipher his one-word answers. The man could just keep himself company for the evening. She might even cajole Adam into giving her a ride home after all.

Christa waved as soon as she caught sight of her friend. After exchanging a warm hug, the two women stood watching the crowd swirl around them.

"You aren't waiting for William, are you?" Ammie finally asked, raising her fan so her voice didn't carry beyond the two of them.

"Of course I am." Christa leaned over and whispered. "I don't suppose you're ready to tell me why you keep trying to warn me off from William. He's really very charming."

Stuck between loyalty to her friend and discretion for her client, Ammie sighed and tried another approach. "What does Adam have to say about him?"

"Why nothing. I don't believe my overly nosy brother is aware of my interest in William." Christa pursed her lips. "And as my best friend, I expect you to keep my confidence."

"Of course," Ammie said automatically. "But I can't believe Adam doesn't know about it."

Christa grinned. "Oh. There are ways to keep secrets from Adam."

Not at all sure how good an idea that was, Ammie bit her

lower lip when William emerged from the crowd along with two of his regular companions. The three men made a beeline for Christa and Ammie, just as the orchestra started playing the first dance of the evening.

For the next several hours Ammie was constantly bombarded with requests for a dance. She graciously turned down most, and concentrated on looking for any short dark-haired men she hadn't met before. She'd spotted one or two, but so far they'd all been vouched for by an acquaintance of hers.

Her feet were starting to hurt, and there was a definite ache creeping up her back, when Adam stepped up beside her. He leaned over to whisper in her ear.

"You're about to get an introduction, Princess."

Nodding her understanding, Ammie continued chatting with their hostess and several other couples as Adam disappeared back into the crowd. A few minutes later, Nathan Milton, William's father who was also one of her clients, joined the group. Ammie's pulse leaped when he was accompanied by a younger man closer to her own age.

He had dark hair and barely topped her in height. When he looked her way, the intensity of his gaze had her drawing in a quick breath. She didn't need to hear the elder Milton's introduction to know that this was the man who Ethan was looking for.

Telling herself to keep calm, both Ethan and Adam were sure to be nearby, she smiled and inclined her head. Seeing her interest, Nathan turned toward her.

"Miss Jamison. I'd like to introduce Mr. Burgess."

The man bowed as she kept a smile in place and her hand firmly clamped around her fan. "Mr. Burgess. I'm happy to make your acquaintance."

The newcomer to the group straightened out and kept

his dark gaze on her face, lingering on each of her features as if he was memorizing them. "The pleasure is mine."

The high, almost whiny voice was at odds with the man's solid build. Ammie raised her fan in a coy gesture that was also effective in hiding her sudden frown. The man's intense stare was forcing her to fight the urge to step away.

As the orchestra started into a new waltz, Mr. Burgess held out his hand. "May I have the honor of a dance?"

Well aware that the man might be keeping company with her father's killer, Ammie stiffened her spine and gave a brief nod. As she placed her hand in his, she sent up a quick prayer of thanks for her gloves.

They'd barely made one turn around the dance floor before her partner leaned back and stared at her. "I've never seen anyone as lovely as you, Miss Jamison. Although there was someone who came close."

Tamping down her revulsion at how near he was to her, Ammie was careful to keep a proper distance between them. "Oh? And who was that, Mr. Burgess?"

"A woman I recently saw during my travels to your interesting city, Miss Jamison. The two of you look very much alike." His lips curled into a slow smile. "As a matter of fact, you could almost be twins, if she hadn't been obviously older than you."

Ammie's feet stopped as she stared at him, but the hard strength in his arm quickly forced her to keep moving. Unwilling to let him see that he was frightening her, Ammie lifted her chin and looked him in the eye.

"How unusual, Mr. Burgess. Did you have an opportunity to talk to this woman?"

His hooded eyes narrowed and she felt his hand on her waist twitch. "No, Miss Jamison. I did not."

He spun them into a dizzying whirl so Ammie had to

concentrate on staying on her feet. She was about to demand her freedom when he suddenly stopped and his arms dropped away as his gaze riveted on a point over her head. A large pair of hands curled around her shoulders and Ammie almost leaned her head back in relief at the feeling of an invisible mantle of protection wrapping itself around her.

Ethan.

"I believe this dance is mine, Ammie."

ETHAN HAD WATCHED the man's introduction to Ammie and then frowned as he led her out onto the dance floor. He hadn't liked it. It had never been his intention to allow this Burgess to get near Ammie, much less put his hands on her. He'd followed their progress, moving to be sure to keep them in sight at all times.

His intent had been to claim her as soon as the dance ended, but that plan had dissolved away the minute he'd seen the distress on her face. Whatever the man had said to her had clearly upset Ammie. And that was more than enough to get his feet moving.

Ignoring the twirling couples around him, Ethan stalked across the floor, coming up behind Ammie and making sure Burgess caught sight of him. When the man had the good sense to stop, Ethan reached out and pulled Ammie away from him.

Ethan watched the shorter man silently, his anger spiking at the rapid rise and fall of Ammie's shoulders beneath his hands. She was frightened, and for that alone, Burgess would pay. When the dark-haired man's gaze raised to his, Ethan didn't even blink.

The two men stared at each other, neither bothering to hide his anger. Ethan had deliberately baited Burgess by using Ammie's given name, making sure the other man understood just who she belonged to. Several tense moments passed as the dancing slowed around them and heads turned to watch the silent drama.

Burgess finally broke off the staring match and stepped away. "Of course." He gave Ammie a slight bow. "Until we meet again, Miss Jamison."

Ethan didn't wait for her response. He turned her around and slipped a hand around her waist. Taking one of her hands in his, he whirled her away from where Burgess stood, glaring after them.

"Are you alright?" He directed the question at her bowed head, waiting patiently for her to raise her eyes to his. When she finally did, he was relieved to see they were clear and bright.

"I'm fine, Ethan." She tightened her hand in his. "Thank you."

"You're welcome." He studied her face for a moment, glad to see the color returning to her cheeks. "What did he say to you?"

She sighed. "He mentioned that he saw Christine. It seems they were on the same train."

Dark eyebrows winged upward in surprise. "They came to San Francisco on the same train?"

"Apparently." Ammie nodded and then gave a slight shudder.

Ethan pulled her an inch closer. "He won't hurt you, Ammie. I won't let him."

Turquoise eyes, the same ones he'd seen in his dreams for eighteen years, met his. Ethan's whole body tightened. She'd always been the most beautiful woman he'd ever met, but even so, he'd never seen her as breath-taking as she was tonight. At that moment, Ethan knew he was holding the entire world in his arms, and he didn't hear or see anything beyond her and the music surrounding them.

As they circled the floor, their bodies moving together, Ethan doubted if he'd ever have a more perfect moment in his life. Wishing that he could kiss her more than he wanted to breathe, he started to lower his head when he suddenly realized the music had stopped.

Still staring up at him, Ammie slowly stepped back, her hand still in his. When the guests broke out into applause, he looked around to find them completely alone in the middle of the room. He grinned at the deep blush blooming across Ammie's cheeks. For once, he wasn't the one turning beet red. Tucking her hand through the crook of his arm, he led her off the dance floor.

And ran right into Adam who was standing with Christa at the edge, watching them. Christa positively glowed at him as she grabbed Ammie's hand.

"Come on. Adam says I'm supposed to take you to get our wraps while he talks to Ethan."

As the blond led a bemused Ammie away, Ethan watched her for a moment before turning a frown on Adam.

"Burgess is here. I need to stay close to Ammie."

Adam shook his head. "You made your intention to stay close to Ammie abundantly clear to the whole company, Ethan. But you don't have to worry about Burgess at the moment. The man has left."

Ethan took a quick look around. "He's left?"

"Something I shouldn't have to tell you since you were supposed to be following him."

Folding his arms across his chest, Ethan shrugged. "He was scaring Ammie."

"Which would only have been a temporary situation, and I'm sure she could have handled it," Adam said. His mouth quirked up at the corners. "But it does bring us back to the same question I asked you earlier."

"What's that, Fromer?"

"How many years have you been in love with Amelia Jamison?"

19

THE FOLLOWING MORNING DAWNED WITH GRAY SKIES AND A faint mist in the air. A sure sign that rain was on its way.

The gloomy weather fit Ethan's mood perfectly as he and Brat made their way to Luke's stables. It was early, and he'd left the house before anyone else had begun to stir. Hoping the hands had made a pot of coffee, and there would still be a couple of horses that needed tending to, Ethan wound his way down the hill and toward the north end of town.

Not in any hurry now that he was out of the house, Ethan kept Brat to a walk as the same thoughts that had plagued him all night continued to pester him in the weak daylight. The intense feeling that the dance with Ammie had awakened just made things worse.

Every minute he'd spend with her would be torture, because nothing had changed. She was Amelia Jamison, born to silk and satin, and he was still Cracker. It was an echo from Shue's words long ago that played constantly in his head.

You're Cracker. You're not like them. You never will be.

The hour was early enough that there were only work wagons making their way through the streets, so it was barely twenty minutes before Ethan rode up to the stable doors which were already open and ready for business. Dismounting outside in the drizzle, Ethan led an eager Brat into the warmer and drier interior.

His horse immediately headed into an empty stall and the feed bucket standing in the corner. One of the hands gave Ethan a friendly wave and with a couple of hand gestures, indicated he'd see to Brat getting fresh water and a little extra feed.

Nodding his thanks, Ethan removed his hat, slapping it against his thigh as he moved toward a back room where the stove, and hopefully a pot of coffee, was located. He only got a few steps inside before he stopped dead, staring at the tall man with the light hair and easy-going air about him, who was pouring a stream of coffee into a tin mug. He turned and smiled at the best tracker around, who was grinning back at him with his hat in his hand.

"Hello, Ethan. Thought I might have to hunt you down when the hour got decent."

His mood considerably lightening at the sight of the man he admired most in this world, Ethan broke out into a wide grin as he gave a hopeful glance around. "Luke. It's good to see you. Are Shannon and the kids with you?"

Ethan's brother-in-law shook his head. "Nope. But they said to say 'hello'. And so did Mudslide."

Catching the speculative look in Luke's eyes, Ethan gave a mental sigh and stepped closer to the stove. He had a pretty good idea why Shannon's husband was here, but he wasn't going to hear it until he'd had a cup of coffee.

Setting his hat on a nearby bench, Ethan reached for another tin mug off the shelf hanging behind the stove. He poured out a good portion and took a long sip before cradling the mug between his hands to warm them up.

"What brings you into town?"

Luke's mouth curved up into the smile that charmed just about anyone around him. "You."

"Let me guess. Shannon sent you."

The rancher chuckled. "What makes you think that?"

Ethan shrugged. "Every wife in the family has sent their husband chasing after me, so it makes sense that Shannon would too."

With amusement lighting up his eyes, Luke laughed. "You're right. She did. But I would have made the trip in without her urging pretty soon anyway. You've been gone awhile."

He paused to take a sip of his coffee. "I guess you're having trouble finding this Hawkes that you told me about?" At Ethan's puzzled look, Luke shrugged. "I stopped at The Crimson Rose last night, expecting you to be staying there. Was surprised when Cook said you'd been staying with Ammie and Charlotte."

He pinned Ethan with a pointed stare. "Can't say that Cook sounded too happy about it."

Ignoring that, Ethan latched onto Luke's comment about Eli Jamison's killer.

"Adam and I figure Hawkes knows he's being hunted, so he's holed up somewhere and not leaving any tracks."

"Adam? He a friend of yours?"

"No," Ethan snorted. "More like a business acquaintance."

"Uh huh. So if this Hawkes isn't showing himself, how do you plan on tracking him down?" Luke set his mug aside and sat down on a nearby chair, stretching his long legs out in front of him.

"He has someone else he's traveling with. A kind of replacement for the ghost killer Charles had a run-in with after his brother was killed." Ethan gave a brief summary of how they'd found Burgess, including the fact he'd stated he'd been on the same train to San Francisco as Christine. When he'd finished, there was a long moment of silence.

"If you're so sure this Burgess is riding with Hawkes, and he was at that party last night, why didn't you follow him then?" Luke asked.

Ethan ran a hand along the side of his cheek. "I was dancing with Ammie."

"Dancing with Ammie?" Luke repeated each word slowly, his gaze never leaving Ethan's face.

"It's kept me awake all night, knowing I should have followed Burgess." Ethan began pacing about the small room. "If I had, we might have Hawkes already, and I'd be headed out."

Luke folded his hands together and rested them on top of his chest as he leaned further back in his chair. "Headed out to where?"

Surprised, Ethan frowned at him. "Back to the ranch, and then out on a stock delivery. I know there's one coming up."

"Uh huh." Luke's calm gaze stayed on his younger brother-in-law. "Why did you dance with Ammie?"

"What?"

"You must have had a reason." Luke shrugged. "What was it?"

"I could tell Burgess was scaring her while they danced." Ethan did another quick turn around the room. Just remembering the look on Ammie's face had his temper stirring.

"I'm guessing you didn't care much for that." Luke waited out Ethan's silence.

Finally giving in, Ethan shook his head. "No. I didn't."

"Or for seeing another man's hands on her."

Luke made the statement in a matter-of-fact voice that Ethan couldn't argue with. "Didn't like that either."

The rancher stood up and rolled his shoulders back and forth before giving Ethan a shrug. "Sometimes a dance is just a dance."

Ethan stood there, staring at Luke while he waged an internal war. Finally making up his mind, he hung his head a little as he took a deep breath. "I went to a tea shop."

Luke's mouth dropped open. "Kate's? You took Ammie to Kate's? Did you go inside and have some tea?"

Nodding, Ethan drew in another breath. "And there was a dress fitting."

Now Luke smiled. "You went to Maggie's shop and waited through one of Ammie's dress fittings?"

"Yes."

Luke walked over and slapped Ethan on the back. "We've all been there, little brother. Not a good place for a man."

Feeling better about his confession, Ethan grinned. "Everything in that place is small. I knocked over a hat rack just trying to walk down the aisle."

"I pushed a whole basket of ribbons off the counter once. It was the last time Maggie let me into her shop." When Ethan laughed, Luke smiled. "But some women are worth sitting in fragile chairs and drinking tea, or spending an hour or two pretending to be interested in a bolt of cloth."

He placed a hand on Ethan's shoulder. "Ammie's that woman for you. Always has been. And running away every few months to deliver horses to the army, or to the ranches up north, hasn't changed that, Ethan."

With the gloom descending on him once again, Ethan blew out a breath. "That's the problem, Luke. Nothing has changed. She's still Amelia Jamison and I'm still that kid no one bothered to name." He looked out past the open door and into the large stable space beyond. "I'll never be anything else, and neither will she."

Startled when all Luke did was snort at that, Ethan gave him a light shove. "You've got a better way of looking at things?"

Easily keeping on his feet, Luke shook his head. "I think you put too much weight on that, Ethan. More weight than Ammie does."

"You don't know that," Ethan scoffed.

Luke simply looked at him with that calm stare of his. "You don't either. Maybe you ought to ask her. And when you do, keep a couple of things in mind."

Curious, Ethan stuck his thumbs under his belt. "What's that?"

"You tend to answer things with as few words as possible, unless you're talking to Ammie."

"We grew up together," Ethan gave by way of an explanation.

"Uh huh. And then there's the other thing." Luke hesitated until Ethan looked at him, and then a wide grin broke out on his face. "You did name your horse after her."

20

"WHY ARE WE LOOKING FOR THIS MR. SANDERS?"

Ammie sighed. She'd already explained it to Ethan, but since it was the first thing he'd said since they'd left the house over an hour ago, she held onto her patience.

"We aren't looking for Mr. Sanders. He's my client. We're looking for his partner who stole a great deal of money from Mr. Sanders."

Ethan made that same sound that half-way between a snort and a sigh, and then when silent again. Ammie kept walking, waiting for him to say something she could actually understand, but he didn't seem to be in the mood to talk tonight. Or at any other time today for that matter.

He hadn't even had one word of protest when she'd shown up in her boy's garb for their late-night outing. He'd also avoided her most of the day, staying near but out of her sight.

It was the same way Ethan had acted after he'd kissed her. And then told her it was a mistake. Now they'd had a dance that had been pure magic, and once again he was acting as if it had been a mistake. The thought was depressing, and had Ammie dragging her feet along the edge of the sand.

She'd led them to an older part of the shoreline where many ships had been abandoned when their crews deserted them to search for gold and silver. This part of the bay was littered with their partially sunk and rotting hulls.

Over the years, fire had regularly devastated the city and the ship graveyards with it. But new hulks continually sailed into the harbor, to be ransacked and abandoned, or turned into a different type of enterprise. Ammie looked out over the quiet beach, stopping to listen. But all she heard was the lap of waves and the creak of waterlogged wood.

Ethan stood beside her, one hand in his coat pocket, the other resting on the handle of his gun as he glanced down the deserted stretch of land and water. "Why did you want to come here?"

"I received word that the partner was seen heading in this direction recently."

He turned his head and peered at her through the darkness. "Word?"

Ammie shivered slightly in the swirling fog and pulled her coat closer around herself.

"This isn't open country, Ethan. You can't follow a set of tracks. A hundred eyes and ears work better." She smiled at that. "Or so Master Kwan has always said."

Ethan looked away before clearing his throat. "Do you spend a lot of time with Master Kwan?"

Surprised by the question, Ammie stared at his averted face. "Quite a bit over the years. Why?"

His gaze dropped to his boots. "I don't know that I like you learning how to fight that way."

Since she could hear the strain in his voice, Ammie leaned over and gave his arm a friendly bump with hers. "It was more learning a way to give me time to run." Ethan lifted his head and frowned at her as she shrugged. "Master Kwan preferred retreat to attack."

When he laughed softly, she smiled. "He also spent most of my lessons teaching me how to move without being seen or heard. He calls it a 'most useful skill'."

"That's good."

Since he sounded much more relaxed, and it didn't appear they would have any luck tracking down Mr. Sanders' thieving partner tonight, Ammie decided to bring up a past she knew he never talked about.

"It's probably a skill you already have."

"What makes you say that?"

"It's something Cracker would have had to learn, I imagine." When he went perfectly still beside her, Ammie sighed. "Slab came by this morning while you were at Luke's stables."

Ethan took a wider stance and crossed his arms over his chest. "And he told you all about Cracker?"

Ammie shook her head. "He felt bad about not telling me that he knew you when I first hired him. And then he said it slipped his mind until you showed up in the square looking for me." She shot him a sideways glance. "And he didn't tell me all about Cracker. I thought maybe you could do that."

He shrugged. "Not much to tell. I left that boy behind long ago."

Thinking there was most likely a piece of Cracker that would never leave Ethan, Ammie smiled. "Is Ethan your given name?"

The silence drew out for so long, Ammie was sure he didn't intend to answer her.

"I doubt it," he finally said.

Her curiosity aroused even more, and not willing to let him off with that short answer, Ammie turned to face him." Why do you doubt it?"

Ethan dropped his arms to his sides and turned to face her as well. The fog swirled around their feet as it drifted by them while they stared at each other.

"I heard the name once and liked the sound of it."

Ammie blinked at that. "What did your parents call you?"

He sighed and rubbed a hand down the side of his cheek. "Cracker. That's what my father called me for as long as I can remember. I never knew my mother. Cook told you the truth. She died in childbirth. At least that's what my father told me."

"Do you believe he was lying to you?"

His broad shoulders lifted into a shrug. "He wasn't particular about telling the truth."

Ammie reached out and laid a hand his arm. "So you had a chance to pick out your own name?"

Ethan looked down at her hand before lifting his gaze back up to hers. "I needed a name when Shannon wanted to make it legal that I was her brother. When she asked, it was the only one I could remember." His mouth curved up at the corners. "I didn't think Slab, or Rabbit, or any of the others I was familiar with would work any better than Cracker."

"Probably not," Ammie laughed. She nodded further down the beach where a few abandoned buildings sat right next to the water. "Let's look a little further down." As they walked, she mulled over the young boy having to come up with a name. "Does Shannon know you chose the name Ethan?"

The tracker shook his head as he matched his steps to hers. "Nope. But I'm sure she suspected it wasn't real."

Ammie let out an inelegant snort at that. "Why isn't it real? It's a name, same as mine. And you don't have to share yours."

"What?"

She kept her gaze steadily on the buildings getting closer as they made their way down the beach. "I was named after Christine's mother. At least, that's what Aunt Charlotte told me. I guess I saw her when I was a little girl, but I don't remember her at all."

"It's a long way to New York, Ammie." Ethan's voice sounded practical, but Ammie wasn't believing it.

"Too long a distance for a letter, I guess." Ammie could hear the pout in her voice, but didn't care. What kind of grandparents hadn't even bothered to contact their only grandchild? Ammie's previous thought about an apple and a tree popped into her head.

"We're a pair, aren't we?" Ammie asked after a long silence. "The boy with no name and the girl her family didn't want?"

They'd almost reached the first building along the beach when Ethan stretched out a hand and stopped her, turning her until she was facing him. "Your family wanted you. Those people in New York aren't family. But everyone here is."

"I could tell you the same thing, Ethan," Ammie said softly.

"You could." When he started to lower his head, Ammie rose up on her toes. Their mouths had barely met when a shot rang out followed by the sound of high-pitched laughter.

~

ETHAN FELT a burning pain along his side. He grunted as he dropped to the ground, dragging Ammie down with him, then rolled his body to be sure he was in between her and the place where he thought the shot had come from.

"Stay still," he whispered into her ear just before a second shot rang out. It whizzed a good two feet over their heads. *Not much on hitting what he aims at.*

Ethan raised his head enough to stare at the abandoned building in front of them. Their attacker might be hiding anywhere inside and shooting through the wide cracks in between the boards precariously holding up the roof.

"He's behind those barrels, to the left of the building."

Ethan's gaze switched over to the area Ammie had whispered to him, watching for any movement or sign of life. There was a slight shift in the darkness, not enough to show a body, but enough to tell Ethan someone was there. At least the fog had smothered the moonlight, so they had that going in their favor.

But then, so did the man shooting at them. It would make it easier for the man to sneak up on them lying out in the open the way they were.

Ethan reached for his gun, just managing to pull it free before another shot rang out, this one much closer, spitting up the sand only a few feet in front of them.

"Can you move?" Ethan barely breathed the words, not wanting them to carry on the night air.

"Give me your gun," Ammie whispered back. When Ethan shook his head, she gently swiped her hand along his side, making him take in a sharp breath of air against the sudden pain.

"You're hurt. I can shoot your gun well enough to keep him down while you crawl to cover."

"I'm not leaving you out here in the open," he hissed at her.

"I'll be right behind you." She moved a few inches away from him. "I'm a smaller target, Ethan. Give me your gun."

Ethan stared at her for several seconds before reluctantly handing it over to her. "It sounds like he has two single-shot pistols. Wait until he fires them both at me, and then you move. And don't fire more than three shots. Save the other three for you getting to cover." He leaned over and placed his lips near her ear. "Promise me, Ammie."

She nodded. Turning onto her stomach, Ammie aimed the pistol. "Go, Ethan."

As Ammie fired, Ethan started a fast, painful crawl toward the shadows of the building, heading for a large gap in the wall. He reached it just as he heard Ammie's third shot. He waited for return fire, but none came.

Hoping Ammie had hit the man and he wasn't simply waiting for her to move, Ethan blinked and almost rubbed his eyes when he saw her make her way up onto the sand-covered walkway running along the side of the building. He barely heard a sound as she crossed over the wooden planks, and was sure what little he could hear wouldn't carry as far as the barrels at the other end of the building.

When she was through the gap and sitting beside him, he took back his gun and reloaded it while he kept an eagle-eye on those barrels.

"Did Master Kwan teach you to move like that?"

There was a white flash of teeth as Ammie smiled. "He did, and he was right. It's a very handy. And so are these special slippers he had made for me."

They waited several minutes, but there was nothing except the gentle lap of waves to break the silence. Gesturing for her to stay where she was, Ethan moved quietly through the building, always keeping the barrels in sight through the gaps in the boards. The closer he got to them, the more he sensed that there was no one hiding there.

He stopped and frowned. This was as far away from Ammie as he was willing to get. Backtracking, he returned to where she was crouching against a wall.

"I think he's gone, but I can't be sure. He might be circling around."

She laid a hand on his arm. "You're hurt, Ethan. We need to get you to a safe place."

Ethan had pressed his bandanna under his shirt and against the wound. The bleeding had already slowed to a trickle. He was fairly certain the bullet had only grazed him, and he'd certainly survived worse wounds than this one. But the loss of blood was making him lightheaded, and the last thing he wanted to do was pass out and leave Ammie completely vulnerable to another attack.

"I know a place nearby," Ammie whispered. "Can you walk a few blocks?"

Thinking it was best if they got away from there, Ethan nodded. "You stay close to me. We'll head through the building and go out the other side closest to the road." He looked up at the sky as the sound of raindrops hit the roof. "Let's move. The rain will give us more cover."

21

Ammie opened the door to what looked like another abandoned house on the edge of the Barbary Coast. When she turned back around, Ethan was leaning against the doorframe, his breathing much heavier than the short walk they'd taken called for.

Slipping an arm around his waist, Ammie urged him inside, guiding him to the only chair next to a wobbly wooden table. He sank down onto it as she hurried back to shut the door against the driving rain. There was a table, one chair, and a candleholder with a stub of a candle in it that was leaning to one side.

Crossing the room to a row of shelves, Ammie reached into the back and came up with a long match. Striking it against the stone of the cold hearth that dominated one wall, she lit the small candle and moved it to the center of the table with its uneven top.

"You've been here before."

She glanced over her shoulder at Ethan. "Yes. I have several places like this where I can go if necessary."

He took a slow look around the single room. "Do you need to come here often?"

She shook her head as she unbuttoned her coat and stepped behind him. "Don't turn around."

"Why?"

Ethan's head started to swivel in her direction, but she stopped him with a firm hand against his cheek.

"Just keep your eyes on the fireplace." Ammie waited until he'd obeyed, then finished taking off her coat and draped it over the back of his chair. She unlaced the ties at her throat, and quickly peeled off her shirt, dropping it over his shoulder and onto his lap.

"What are you doing, Ammie?"

She rolled her eyes at his sharp tone as she reached for her coat. Thrusting her arms through the sleeves, she made short work of buttoning it back up all the way to her chin. Stepping in front of him, she put her hands on her hips and shook her head. "I'm going to make you a bandage."

He frowned at the shirt lying across his legs. "You could have used my shirt."

"You didn't have your coat buttoned, so it's filthy from crawling through the sand and dirt." Ammie shrugged. "Not to mention bloody." She held out her hand. "My shirt please, and the knife you carry behind your back."

He grimaced as he twisted to retrieve the knife, but managed to put it into her outstretched hand.

Ammie sat on the floor and started to cut long strips from her shirt. When she had several, she took the rest of the destroyed garment and went to the door, holding it out into the rain until it was thoroughly soaked. Plopping the wet rag onto the table, she knelt in front of Ethan intending to undo the buttons of his coat.

"I can do it."

He raised his hands, but she brushed them aside. "Sit still. You'll just have to take my help."

Ammie worked at getting his coat off and then reached for the laces at his neck. Loosening them, she carefully inched the shirt upward, wincing when she had to pick the material away from his wound. She was sure she was hurting him, but through it all, Ethan didn't make a sound. When she peeked at his face, he was watching her intently, a faint smile on his mouth.

"Am I hurting you?"

"No."

She wasn't sure she believed him, but doggedly kept at it until she had his shirt over his head and free of his arms. With a huge sigh of relief, Ammie carried the bloody garment to the front door and draped it across a log just to the side, hoping the rain would wash most of the blood out.

When she returned to Ethan, he'd already picked up the wet cloth and was dabbing at his wound. She dropped to her knees again and gently took over the task, biting her lip as she concentrated on cleaning out the slowly oozing gash.

She turned a worried gaze up to his. "Maybe I should go for Dr. Abby?"

He immediately shook his head. "It isn't that bad. And you aren't crossing the Barbary Coast by yourself in the rain. Your coat and boots would be enough to kill for."

Ammie thought that was going a bit too far, but she didn't want to argue with him. Picking up the cloth strips, she began to carefully wind them around his middle, trying not to stare at the hard muscles all across his arms and chest. Her breathing was noticeably faster by the time she'd tied off the ends, and she was very glad to be able to stand and take a long step away from him.

"I hope that will hold until we can leave."

Just then, it sounded like a bucket of nails fell onto the roof as the rain increased to a pounding intensity.

"Which may not be any time soon," Ethan said.

Silently agreeing with him, Ammie stifled a yawn. Her pocket watch said it was well after midnight, and suddenly she felt as if all the energy had drained right out of her. And judging by the droop in Ethan's shoulders, he was feeling the same way.

The chill of the room began to seep through her coat, and there wasn't any wood to start a fire even if she was willing to risk one in the crumbling hearth. Thinking there was nothing to do but make the best of it, Ammie reached over and grabbed one of Ethan's hands. Tugging on it, she frowned when he only looked up at her.

"What are you doing?"

"Trying to get you to your feet. There's a nice pile of hay over there with a good blanket over it to keep the straws from sticking in your back. You need to lie down."

Ethan glanced over to the corner. "You lie down. I'll be fine right here."

"No one's going to barge through that door tonight, Ethan. And not a soul living in the coast gets up before noontime. They're just as bad as the society ladies. Come on. I'll barricade the chair against the door if it will make you feel better." She gave another pull on his hand but he still didn't budge. She stood back and glared at him. "Ethan. It's late and I'm tired."

"Fine. I give up." He pushed himself to a standing position and draped a heavy arm over her shoulders. "Help me over there."

Ammie staggered a step or two under his weight, but she finally got him to the crude bed of straw. He lay down on his back while she tugged his boots off, and then went to drag the chair over to the door. Ammie carefully tipped it against the wood so that any movement would send it toppling to the floor.

"Not much of a barricade," Ethan noted as she returned to where he was lying, watching her through half-closed lids.

She shrugged as she sat on the edge of the straw to unlace her shoes. "It will make a noise."

Shaking his head, he placed his gun and his knife next to him on the straw, then whipped out a hand and latched onto one of Ammie's. With a swift tug, he had her off-balance and tumbling sideways. Ammie let out a squeak. She dropped her last shoe when Ethan wrapped long arms around her and softened her fall by pulling her down onto his chest.

It took Ammie a moment to realize she was sprawled out all over him. And the man seemed to throw off more heat than a cozy fire.

"Your hands are like ice." His amused voice sounded from somewhere over her head.

They feel that way too, Ammie thought, but she only shrugged. "It's cold." She struggled to sit up, but his arms were like bands of iron keeping her in place. "What are you doing, Ethan? Let me up."

"No. I'm keeping you warm."

"But..." She was speechless when he dropped a soft kiss into her hair.

"Go to sleep."

Not likely.

That was Ammie's last thought as her eyes closed and she dropped into a peaceful sleep.

~

ETHAN'S EYES popped open at the loud boom of thunder, followed immediately by a crack of lightning so bright it lit up the shabby room. He'd started to reach for his gun before he realized there was an unfamiliar weight on his shoulder. Ammie snuggled closer, and he felt the slight tremble in her shoulders.

He put a finger under her chin and lifted it as he tipped his own down. Ethan was surprised when she cringed at another clap of thunder. It wouldn't have occurred to him that his usually brash, sometimes reckless Ammie was afraid of a little thunder and lightning.

When another bolt sizzled through the air with a loud crack, he grinned. All right. A lot of thunder and lightning. "The storm sounds like it's directly over us." He ran a gentle hand over her shoulder. "They move pretty fast. It'll pass in no time."

"I know." Her voice was small as she visibly tensed for the next roll of thunder. "It's silly, but I've always been afraid of storms. Uncle Charles thinks it's because we went through a bad one on the voyage here when I was very little." She sighed. "He said it was the same storm when Papa broke his ankle."

"When you were growing up, did you spend all the stormy nights in your Aunt Charlotte's bed?" Ethan smiled at the picture that made.

Ammie laughed. "Yes, I did. And now instead of me running down the hallway, she usually comes to my bedchamber and tells me stories about her life on the plantation, and all the mischief her brothers used to get into."

"She still does that?" Ethan threaded his fingers through her hair which had escaped its tie and was flowing softly down her back. He liked the feel of it beneath his hand.

Shrugging, Ammie ducked her head. "It helps if I have a distraction."

Ethan gently moved her off his chest until she was flat on her back, staring up at him with wide eyes. He bent his elbow and propped his head on his hand as he grinned at her. "Is that so? Well. I don't have any objections to distracting you."

She only had time to blink before he lowered his head and laid his lips on hers. He moved his mouth gently back and forth until her breathing quickened and her lips opened up for him. The minute they did, his tongue swept inside, exploring every inch as he claimed it for his own.

When she groaned deep in her throat, he broke off the kiss and trailed his mouth across her heated cheek and down her neck, lingering there as one of his hands unbuttoned her coat and peeled the straps of her chemise down to her waist, before making a slow path back up her ribcage. When his hand finally covered a full breast, it was his turn to groan as he palmed the soft mound.

Ethan's mouth continued its assault downward, pausing only when he felt her hands glide through his hair. Kissing a path over the slope of her other breast, he didn't stop his movement until he'd taken a rigid nipple into his mouth.

"Ethan!" Ammie gasping out his name only made him smile. He continued to kiss and explore for several more minutes before he raised his head and slid back up her body, letting her feel the hard muscles of his chest against her much softer skin. He cradled her face with his hands and kissed her until she was squirming beneath him.

Rising up, he smiled down at her. "I told you, Ammie. I give up. I don't have any fight left in me. You've been mine since the day I laid eyes on you." He leaned down for another long kiss, then laid his forehead against hers. "Tell me you know that."

"I know it, Ethan," she said softly. "I've always known it. But..."

Her voice trailed off when his hand went to the rope tied around her waist. "Tell me you're mine."

She wrapped her arms around his neck and kissed him until his head began to spin. Ethan's hands got busy as he stripped them both out of the rest of their clothes and carefully settled himself on top of her.

He closed his eyes at the exquisite sensation of her lying naked under him.

In his wildest dreams he'd never thought it would feel like this. His heart pounded as he slowly eased into her, his breathing growing harsher with every second as he fought for control. When they were completely joined, he laid his head on her shoulder, grimacing with the intense feeling that bloomed when she moved restlessly beneath him and her lips grazed against his ear.

"I love you, Ethan."

The soft words were his undoing. Not waiting a second more, he began to carefully move, taking them both into a world where there was nothing but pleasure and the two of them.

22

ETHAN CAME WIDE AWAKE ALL AT ONCE. SITTING UP, HE braced his arms behind him as he looked around, shaking his head to chase away the last of the sleep. When his gaze fell on the empty space next to him, he froze. His eyes darted around the room, looking for Ammie, but she wasn't there. The chair she'd propped by the door the night before was now placed beside the table, and his shirt was hanging off the back.

Frowning, Ethan checked to be sure his gun was still where he'd left it, before he reached over and retrieved his pants from the floor just beyond the edge of the hay. It only took him a few minutes to get decent enough.

He was pulling on his second boot when the door to their refuge opened and Ammie appeared. She had a tin plate covered with a cloth in her hand, and a canteen hung from a strap around her shoulder.

She smiled at him as she shoved the door shut with the toe of her shoe. "Good morning. I thought you might need something to eat."

Ethan glanced over at the closed door and then back at Ammie. "You went out to get food?"

Nodding, she set the plate on the table along with the canteen. "It isn't much, but it should hold you until we can get home for a proper breakfast." She gave him a stern look. "After we've seen Doctor Abby."

He stomped his foot to push his last boot into place, then stood and crossed his arms over his still-bare chest. "You shouldn't have gone out alone."

"I was fine. Just as I told you, there wasn't a soul stirring anywhere." She pointed at the chair. "At least sit and eat while you lecture me."

"I don't lecture," Ethan grumbled, but he relented and walked over to the table. Lifting the cloth, he was surprised to see four fluffy buttermilk biscuits on the plate. "Where did you get them?"

"Mama Lou's." When he said nothing, Ammie gave him a cheeky smile. "She has a whorehouse not far from here, and always has biscuits before she retires for the evening, which is usually just around dawn."

Sighing, Ethan rubbed a hand along his cheek. Now how would Amelia Jamison know something like that?

"A hundred eyes and ears, Ethan, remember? I told you that last night."

"I remember everything about last night." He pointed at the chair while he admired the becoming blush on her cheeks. "You sit. I'm used to eating standing up." When she raised a skeptical eyebrow, he grinned at her. "And eating while sitting on the back of a horse. It's all part of ranch life."

Ammie nodded and took the seat. Reaching for a single biscuit she broke it in half. She pushed the rest of the tin toward Ethan, who'd walked over to the opposite side of the table.

Ethan stared at the half-biscuit in front of her. "Is that all you're going to eat?"

"We really aren't discussing that again, are we?"

He had a suspicion they'd be talking about how much she didn't eat for a lot of years to come. Remembering what was at the top of the mental list of things he needed to do today, he picked up a biscuit and took a big bite, chewing while he kept his gaze on Ammie.

She finally lifted her chin and stared back at him. "What is it?"

He hesitated, not sure he wanted to disrupt the private world they'd made for themselves. But they couldn't stay in their rundown piece of heaven forever, and there were some things they needed to get straight between them.

"Are you sorry about last night?" He braced himself, half-expecting her to say that she was.

Ammie froze with the biscuit still in her hand. She put it back onto the plate before raising her gaze to his. "No. And if you are, then I'd appreciate it if you'd keep it to yourself."

Startled that she'd think such a thing, Ethan frowned. "I'm not sorry."

"You were after our kiss, and then again after our dance."

Ethan's eyebrows shot up. "Sorry? I wasn't sorry."

She sighed and looked down at the tabletop. "You said it was a mistake."

He squatted down next to her chair and lifted her chin with one finger until he was looking into eyes slightly misted with tears. "It was a mistake because you are who you are, and I can't change who I am. But I was never sorry."

"Who are you, Ethan?"

He sighed and stood up, retreating to his usual spot near

the fireplace. "A man who grew up mostly in back alleys, lying and stealing for a living."

Ammie's mouth dropped to her chest. "Lyng and stealing for a living? Ethan, you cannot be serious. You were only a child trying to survive."

"Maybe so," Ethan conceded. "But I'm still from the back alleys and you're still the girl from the big house on the hill."

She let out a short laugh. "The girl whose mother didn't want her, or even give her a thought over the years."

Annoyed that Ammie would allow someone as shallow and selfish as Christine Jamison Aldrin to have any kind of influence on her, Ethan covered the short distance to the table and lifted her right up out of the chair. "She's nothing compared to you, Ammie. And the biggest fool alive. Everyone who's ever met you loves you."

Her expression softened as she looked up at him. "Does that include you, Ethan?"

He was helpless to deny it, and wouldn't have even if he'd had the strength. She needed to hear the words, and he needed to say them to her.

"It does. I love you, Amelia Jamison. I always have." He pulled her closer and put his lips on hers, moving them softly against her mouth before raising his head to stare down into the most beautiful eyes he'd ever seen.

"You're sure my past doesn't matter to you?"

He smiled and lifted a hand to run a finger down her soft cheek. "You don't have a past, sweetheart. And you had no hand in what happened all those years ago. It's over and doesn't mean a damn thing to me, and it shouldn't to you either."

She rose on her toes and kissed him. Just as his arms tightened around her and he was thinking about finding that pile of hay again, she lifted her head and smiled. "I would say the same thing to you, Ethan. Your past simply doesn't matter any more."

He opened his mouth then shut it again. Holding her in his arms, he wanted to believe that. And maybe she was right. But it didn't really matter if she was or not. He loved her and was never going to let her go again.

Feeling more at peace than he ever had in his entire life. Suddenly famished, Ethan grinned as he leaned over and grabbed another biscuit. "There's something we have to do this morning."

She shook her head. "Whatever it is, I need to go home and have a hot bath first. I could hear noises underneath that straw we slept on."

Ethan lifted his hand and pointed his second biscuit at her. "Which is why we have to do this first."

"Do what, Ethan? I'm tired, and dirty, and I'd like to go home if it isn't too much of a bother."

He set his half-eaten breakfast down and reached over to grab her hand, drawing her out of the chair. "That's fine. Let's get going."

"But we haven't finished..."

He kept pulling her along behind him. "We'll get something to eat later."

"First you complain about me not eating enough, and now you won't let me eat at all."

To keep her feet from digging in, Ethan used the one argument he knew she'd go along with. "We don't want Charlotte and Helen worrying about us."

"I sent one of the young boys who does chores at Mama Lou's off with a note. They won't be worried."

So much for that. Ethan kept moving, heading down one quiet street and then another with a protesting Ammie dragging along behind him.

"Are you intending for us to walk all the way home?" Her grumpy tone was all he needed to hear to know what kind of mood she was in. "And if it's of any interest to you, you're headed in the wrong direction."

"I promise to get you a hot bath and a good meal soon, sweetheart. Trust me to take care of you." Ethan stopped when they crossed Market Street and turned left.

He had a good idea where to go, but was relieved to spot the small church with its makeshift steeple down a side street. Heading in that direction he didn't stop until he was standing on the steps in front of the two wooden doors leading inside.

"Here?" Ammie tugged on her hand until he let go. "This is where you wanted to go?" She looked from the wooden cross hanging on the door over to Ethan. "Why?"

"I know the preacher. I figured he wouldn't mind us waking him up so early."

Ammie's eyes narrowed and her hands went to her hips as her foot started rapidly tapping against the stone step. "Why do we need a preacher?"

Ethan crossed his arms over his chest and stared right back at her. This was one argument he was not going to lose. "We're getting married."

"Not right now we aren't," Ammie shot back.

"Yes, right now." He quirked an eyebrow at her. "We've had relations, Ammie. It might be putting the carriage in front of the horse, but as long as we've got both of them, we'll be fine."

Ammie's eyes shot wide open, and she stepped forward to place her hand over his mouth. "I cannot believe you are standing on the steps of a church and talking about such a thing."

He reached up and removed her hand but kept it in his. "You said you loved me."

"Well, yes, but..."

Now he put his big hand gently over her mouth. "And I told you I love you too. Nothing is going to keep me from marrying you right now. I need you to do this, Ammie."

When he carefully removed his hand, she took in a deep breath. "But Ethan..."

Deciding on another plan to persuade her, Ethan lowered his head and covered her mouth with his. When she finally relented and wound her arms around his neck, he took a few more seconds to enjoy the feel of her body against his before lifting his head and smiling at her. Running a finger down her soft cheek, he wiggled his eyebrows. "Now that's something you shouldn't do on a church step unless you're man and wife." He smiled at her. "Or about to be." Ethan unwound her arms and tucked one of her hands securely into his.

Walking up the final step, he pulled on the heavy door, relieved when it opened with only a loud creak of its hinges. Stepping inside he looked around the compact space, and grinned when he saw a pair of feet sticking out from the end of one of the pews. Pulling Ammie along, he walked over and prodded one of the feet with his free hand.

"Rabbit, wake up. I've got some preacher business for you to do."

A head with a mop of black hair flanked by two ears sticking straight out, appeared above the back of the pew. "What? Who's there?" the head disappeared and then reappeared, wearing a pair of spectacles. Two eyes squinted at Ethan from behind the lenses.

"Cracker? Is that you?"

"Sure is. I hear you're a preacher, Rabbit."

"Jacob. Everyone calls me Jacob now." He peered over at Ammie and his eyes grew wider behind his glasses. "Who is this?"

"Amelia Jamison." Ethan waited while the name sunk in. Given the newly-designated Jacob's prior life of robbing the customers leaving the gaming houses, it wasn't likely he'd miss the significance of Ammie's name.

She bowed her head. "It's nice to meet you, Reverend Jacob."

He smiled at her before he had to stifle a yawn. "Everyone just calls me Preacher, Miss Jami..." Jacob stopped in mid-sentence and turned a bit pale. He glanced over at Ethan. "Did you say Jamison?"

"Yep," Ethan confirmed. "Charles Jamison's niece."

The preacher immediately did a comical scramble to his feet and straightened out his robe. "Miss Jamison, it's a pleasure." He bowed so low his head smacked against the seat of the pew. He rubbed the red spot that appeared as he looked at Ethan. "What are you doing here at this hour, and with Charles Jamison's niece?"

"Amelia and I need to get married."

Jacob's face went even more pale. "Need to?"

"Want to," Ethan hastily amended. "We want to get married."

Pursing his lips, Jacob looked from one to the other. "Right now?"

"Yes."

The preacher frowned at Ethan and turned his attention to Amelia. "What about you, Miss Jamison? Do you want to get married right now too?"

Ethan held his breath then slowly let it out when Ammie answered with a soft "yes".

Jacob still didn't look convinced. "Well, if you're both sure."

"We are," Ethan cut in. He took the two ten-dollar gold pieces he always carried with him for good luck out of his pocket and held them up for his old friend to see. When Jacob's eyes took on a gleam, Ethan smiled to himself. Fortunately for him, some things never changed.

"Well then." The preacher cleared his throat and stepped out into the narrow aisle. "We'd better get started."

AN HOUR LATER, Ethan and Ammie walked hand-in-hand up the steps to the stately brick home set back from a quiet tree-lined street. Ammie's big smile was at odds with Ethan's mood. Inside him was a confusing mixture of pure happiness and terror.

Being Ammie's husband had him walking on air, but the thought of facing Charles Jamison with the unexpected news that he and Ammie were married, made him want to look around for a safe place to hide. Ethan had no illusions that the man who'd been part of his extended family for two decades would spare him the brunt of his anger over this sudden union, no matter how optimistic Ammie was about her uncle's reaction.

Or her aunt's. Ethan had seen how the women reacted when there wasn't a proper proposal or ceremony. And he hadn't given his new bride either one.

Too late now for regrets he didn't feel anyway, Ethan squared his shoulders and followed Ammie into the house that he'd been in hundreds of times before. Just never as Ammie's husband. He didn't have long to ponder the matter since Lillian immediately emerged from the parlor.

"I wasn't expecting company so early in the day." She smiled. "The children are off to a lesson with Master Kwan. If I had known you'd both be coming by, I'd have kept them at home." She walked over and gave Ammie a kiss on her cheek. "They love seeing you, especially Sarah."

Lillian stepped back and frowned. Her gaze shifted between the two of them as she tilted her head to the side. "What's wrong?"

Ethan cleared his throat. "Nothing. We have something to tell you." Having gotten that far, Ethan couldn't seem to get another word out.

"Oh?" Lillian's attention centered on Ammie as she studied her niece's face. "You got married."

"What?" Ethan's mouth dropped open as Ammie laughed and threw her arms around her aunt.

"Yes."

Lillian looked over Ammie's shoulder as she returned the excited bride's hug. Ethan could see both a clear question and a warning in her crystal-blue gaze. The older woman finally managed to step back and slip an arm around Ammie's waist. "Both of you go in and get comfortable while I arrange for tea and coffee."

Ethan would have preferred something a lot stronger, but he silently nodded as he urged Ammie into the tastefully decorated parlor with its muted colors and elegant touches of dark wood. While Ammie settled into a roomy chair, Ethan stood next to her, taking his usual stance next to the fireplace.

Lillian came back into the room a few minutes later, selecting a seat across from Ammie. Folding her hands in her lap, she looked at her niece. "Well? When did this all happen?"

"This morning." Ammie looked up and smiled at Ethan.

From the corner of his eye, he saw one of Lillian's eyebrows wing up as she glanced at the clock ticking away on the mantel behind him.

"I see." Ammie's aunt turned a calm gaze on him. "Did Charlotte give you her blessing?"

He shifted uncomfortably at the backhanded reminder of something else he hadn't gotten around to yet. He managed to shake his head just as the housekeeper bustled in with a heavily laden tray in her hands.

Grateful for the distraction, Ethan kept his silence as the women busied themselves pouring out tea and coffee. He nodded his thanks when Ammie handed him a sturdy mug, hoping the hot drink would help calm his nerves.

It seemed to him that the ritual of pouring out a couple of cups of tea and handing them around was taking twice as long as usual, but Lillian finally nodded at her housekeeper. The woman had barely exited the room when the front door opened and several pairs of boot steps rang across the large foyer.

"Lillian?" Charles' voice rolled through the open doorway. "Where are you?"

"In the parlor," Lillian called out before turning a smile on Ethan. "I thought it would save time if Amelia's uncle was also present for this discussion."

"Wonderful!" Ammie clapped her hands together as a leaden ball of dread formed in the pit of Ethan's stomach.

At that moment, he'd rather face a dozen Mudslides rather than his wife's uncle. He braced himself as Charles strode through the door and then almost groaned when Cook and Luke came in right behind him.

23

Ammie leaped out of her chair and ran across the room. Charles caught his niece in a fierce hug, a huge smile on his face.

"We have wonderful news, Uncle Charles."

He glanced over at Lillian and his smile began to fade. Holding Ammie off with one arm, he looked down at her. "What news is that?"

"Ethan and I are married." She reached up and laid a hand alongside her uncle's cheek. "And I couldn't be happier. I hope you'll remember that when you're having your talk with him." She leaned to the side and looked at Cook who'd folded his long arms across his chest and was boring a hole into Ethan with his stare. "Both of you."

Cook only grunted as Charles shifted his gaze from his wife to Ethan.

"I'll try." Charles let her go so she could give a hug to Cook and Luke.

Ethan took a quick glance in Luke's direction. His brother-in-law was staring back at him as if he'd lost his mind. Ethan sighed and rubbed a hand along the side of his cheek.

Maybe he had, but he still didn't regret a second of his time with Ammie. He just hoped they wouldn't insist that it was the last he'd see of her. He'd hate to have to give a thrashing to all three men to make his point that he was serious about being her husband.

"It would be best if we retired to my study."

Charles' flat statement had Ethan stiffening his posture.

"I'm coming along," Cook said, a hint of anger slicing through his voice.

"Me too." Luke sounded calmer but just as determined.

Sighing, Ethan nodded as Ammie crossed the room and came to stand beside him. She slipped a slender arm around his waist and frowned at the three men staring back at Ethan.

"So am I."

Appreciating her firm show of support, Ethan smiled at her but shook his head. "Not this time, sweetheart." He leaned down and gave her a brief kiss on the mouth. "Why don't you go and have that bath while I talk to your uncle."

Lillian rose from her seat and reached a hand out toward Ammie. "An excellent idea. You can't keep Ethan from getting the dressing down he deserves, so we may as well make the most of our time. While you're bathing, we can plan an informal dinner party for this evening."

Ammie frowned. "And during my bath will I also be getting *my* dressing down from you?"

Her aunt laughed. "Depend on it."

His bride gave Ethan a reassuring squeeze around his waist before unwinding her arm and leaving with Lillian. She sent him one last look of encouragement over her shoulder before she stepped out of his sight. Since there was no help for it, and wanting to get it over with, Ethan inclined his head toward the parlor door.

"Your study?"

The gambler nodded. "I believe you know the way."

A few minutes later, Ethan found himself sitting in a deep leather chair facing Charles, who'd taken a seat behind his large mahogany desk. Luke and Cook stood on either side of the gambler, and both crossed their arms over their chests as they fixed their stare on Ethan's face.

"I'm assuming Ammie was stating a fact when she said the two of you were married?" Charles began, waiting for Ethan's quiet agreement. "Did this marriage take place last night?"

Ethan resisted the urge to squirm in his seat the way he had when he was younger and was facing the wrath of one of the many uncles in the family. "No."

"It's early, Ethan," Cook put in. "Not quite noon yet. Are you telling us that you and Ammie woke up and decided to get married first thing this morning in Charlotte's parlor?" He didn't wait for a response before growling, "why the hurry?"

A wave of heat crashed through Ethan's body, and he could feel the sweat already forming on his brow. "Not in in the parlor?"

Charles frowned. "What does that mean?"

Clearing his throat, Ethan tried again. "We didn't get married in Charlotte's parlor."

"Where then?" Charles snapped out.

"In a church off Market Street."

Cook snorted at that. "Didn't see any carriage outside. How'd you get from Market Street to here?"

The heat wave got even hotter as Ethan stared at the men who'd helped raise Ammie. "We walked."

As both Charles and Cook sputtered, Luke held up a hand. "Let's have the whole story, Ethan. You must have had a reason for going off and marrying Ammie without getting her uncle's blessing first?"

Sidestepping Luke's question, Ethan started explaining about seeking out his old friend-turned-preacher, painting the simple ceremony in more glowing terms than it probably deserved. When he finally wound down, Charles was drumming his fingers on the top of his desk. "I'm still waiting to hear why all the haste."

Ethan had already worked out that explanation during the long walk from Market Street. "Ammie and I went out to look for a man who'd embezzled money from a client of hers."

"I told her not to take on that client," Cook grumbled before waving a hand at Ethan. "Go on."

"We were down near the wrecked ships when we were shot at."

Luke dropped his arms and leaned against the desk. "Shot at? By who?"

"I don't know and didn't stop to ask. I just wanted to get Ammie away from there."

Charles sucked in a loud breath. "Were either of you hurt?"

"She wasn't."

Luke narrowed his eyes and gave Ethan a quick once-over. "How about you?"

"A graze in my side. Nothing serious, but I lost enough blood I needed to rest up a bit." Ethan thought that sounded reasonable enough, and was relieved when all three men's expressions eased off some.

"Hard rain last night. Wouldn't have been easy to get you home in that."

Nodding his agreement, Ethan gave his brother-in-law a grateful look.

Charles leaned back in his chair and studied the man in front of him. "Why were you married this morning, Ethan?" he asked quietly.

"I love Ammie." Ethan's simple statement had Cook's mouth curving up. "I always have. I could have lost her last night, and I..." he stopped when the words wouldn't come. "I..."

"We all understand, Ethan." Luke smiled at him before turning his gaze on the other two men. "Don't we?"

Blowing out a long breath, Charles ran a hand through his hair. "I want to understand what you're saying here, Ethan. You and Ammie were shot at last night. You managed to get her away safely, which I'm very grateful for, but you were hurt so you had to hole up all night somewhere in the Barbary Coast because you needed rest, and the two of you didn't want to get soaked in the rain. Then after this eye-opening experience, you both decided to get married, and you walked her over to Market Street and to have a ceremony performed by a man named Rabbit..."

"Jacob," Ethan quickly put in. "He goes by Jacob now."

"Don't interrupt your elders, son," Cook said before nodding at Charles to continue.

"All right then," Ammie's uncle shrugged. "By a man named Jacob. And then you walked her over to my home to inform her aunt and I about this marriage." He sat back and kept drumming his fingers on the desk. "I assume you are aware that you left quite a number of important items off your list of things to do before presuming to marry my niece?"

"Yes, sir." Ethan was only too aware of that, but there was one thing he could rectify right now. "I know I haven't done this right, and I apologize for that. But I'd like to ask for Amelia's hand in marriage, and your blessing for our union." He rubbed his palms against the sides of his pants. "I love her, and I'll do everything a man can do to make her happy and provide her with a home she can be proud of." Ethan drew in a quick breath. "I realize I'm not good enough for her, but I'll spend every waking moment..."

Charles cut him off by holding up a hand and rolling his eyes. "I believe that's the longest speech I've ever heard out of you, but you can spare us the rest of it, Ethan. I wouldn't believe any of that load of dung you've always carried around about not being as good as we are anyway."

He sighed at Ethan's stunned look. "Since the deed is done, I suppose I have no choice but to give my blessing." He sent Cook a rueful grin. "And to keep us from having to beat some sense into him, although I reserve the right to change my mind."

Luke snorted out a laugh while Ethan couldn't get a word out around his huge smile. When Charles held out his hand, Ethan jumped out of his chair to grab it.

"Thank you, sir."

His new father-in-law shook his head. "This truly is an occasion to remember." He raised an eyebrow at Luke. "Has he ever called you 'sir'?"

The rancher gave the gambler who was also a long-time friend, as well as an extended family member, an easy-going smile. "Not that I recall."

~

IT WAS LATE when Ethan and Ammie waved goodbye to the crowd gathered on the porch of Lillian and Charles' home. The sounds of Charlotte and Helen's happy sobs could be heard above the calls for well-wishes as the couple made their way to the horse and carriage waiting by the curb.

"It was kind of Uncle Charles to give us a way home other than walking." Ammie teased as Ethan handed her into the carriage.

"It's a lot easier," Ethan agreed. He took up the reins and set the horse into motion before turning to look at his bride. "And I do appreciate Charlotte and Helen leaving us alone in the house tonight."

"Oh?" Ammie trailed a finger along his arm. "Why is that, Mr. Mayes?"

He grinned at her. "No particular reason, Mrs. Mayes. Thought we'd both enjoy some peace and quiet after all the ruckus today."

She laughed, the sound sending a warmth through his veins.

"You consider our wedding supper more of a ruckus than being shot at?"

Ethan shook his head. "Nope. Can't say that." He frowned. "Wish I knew who was behind that gun last night."

"Mr. Burgess," Ammie said around a yawn, drawing a surprised look from her husband.

"How do you know that?"

"I heard him. He has a very particular voice."

Remembering the high-pitched laughter as the first shot had been fired, Ethan turned it over in his mind. "You're sure?" he asked slowly.

Ammie nodded. "I am." She gave him a questioning look when he fell silent. "What is it?"

"I'm wondering how he happened to be where we were last night. He didn't follow us. I'd stake my life on that."

"I don't know." Ammie chewed on her lower lip. "A strange coincidence."

"Too much of a coincidence," Ethan said.

"It's a good place to hide," his wife said softly. She placed a hand on his sleeve and looked up at him. "Only Burgess wouldn't need a hiding place."

"But Hawkes does," Ethan finished her thought out loud. "I'll take Slab tomorrow and have a look around."

"*We'll* take Slab," Ammie insisted, then frowned when he shook his head.

"No, Ammie. We might have to search through those ships and it's too dangerous. I won't risk you that way."

"It isn't your risk to take, Ethan."

They were still arguing about it when Ethan pulled into the carriage house. He climbed out and went around to help Ammie.

When she suddenly gasped, he followed his instinct and whirled around just as two men moved out of the shadows and leaped at him. Keeping in front of his wife, Ethan's arm drew back in a flash and connected hard with the jaw of the man closest to him. He went down with a howl of pain as Ethan pivoted to face the second one when a sweet odor reached out from behind him.

A sudden lightheadedness had him grabbing for the side of the carriage as he felt Ammie slump against his back. Spinning around, he caught her in his arms and broke her fall as he sank to his knees.

"Well, I guess we'll jist bring him along so he can carry his wife." The tallest man of the three reached over and lifted Ethan's gun from its holster, and then the knife strapped next to the small of his back.

Ethan violently shook his head, trying to clear it as he pulled Ammie closer to his chest.

"We weren't told nothin' about bringin' along a man. Jist the woman."

Taking several deep breaths, Ethan's head began to clear. He looked up at the two men standing over them, only to find himself staring into the barrel of a gun.

"Well I ain't dragging her and Shorty over to the wagon, and we cain't leave neither of them here." When Ethan moved his legs, the man holding the gun waved it in his face. "Now you can either pick up the woman and come quiet-like. Or I can shoot you right here." His lips pulled back to show a row of rotting teeth. "Of course, that bullet might hit her too."

Without a word, Ethan slowly got to his feet, still cradling Ammie in his arms. When the gun waved toward the open door of the stable, he walked out into the night.

24

Ethan carefully held Ammie, counting every breath she took. He didn't know what had caused her to collapse into a boneless heap, but it had him numb with worry. As the wagon rattled its way through the dark streets, Ethan kept an unblinking eye on his wife, willing her to wake up and say his name.

His head jerked when the wheels ground to a halt. Looking over the raised edge of the wagon, he somehow wasn't surprised to see the same stretch of dirt and sand that he and Ammie had walked over the night before. And beyond it rose the dark outlines of the wrecked hulks of a hundred ships.

The soft clink of metal against metal grew louder as a dark figure, wearing a long cloak with the hood pulled up to conceal his face, walked into view. He carried a small bag in one hand, and in the other was a revolver pointed right at Ethan.

"Who's this?" The deep, slightly raspy voice held more curiosity than annoyance.

"He came with her." The leader of the threesome who'd

kidnapped Ethan and Ammie, jumped down from the seat of the wagon and sauntered toward the back.

The dark figure kept his gun aimed into the wagon as he shrugged. “Our bargain didn’t include a man.”

The leader shrugged as well. “He wouldn’t let go of her. I couldn’t shoot him without hitting her, and you said she had to be alive.”

“The same dilemma that I am now facing.” The stranger tossed the bag he was carrying toward the road. It landed on the still-soggy ground with a dull thud. “There’s your payment. Take it, and the rest of your friends, and don’t come back. Our business is concluded.”

“What about the wagon? Shorty’s hurt.” The large man pointed an accusatory finger at Ethan. “He broke Shorty’s jaw.”

“Unfortunate for your friend. I suggest you start walking so you can find him a comfortable place to rest.” The dark figure shook his head. “Consider the horse and wagon penance for bringing me an additional problem to deal with.”

Stalking over to where the bag lay, the leader picked it up and weighed it carefully in his hand before gesturing to the two men standing off to the side. “C’mon then.”

Once they’d staggered off, with two of them supporting the hapless Shorty between them, the cloaked figure flipped back the hood of his garment and stared at Ethan. He wasn’t tall, but stood ramrod straight as he stepped closer to the back of the wagon bed.

“I’m well aware of who *she* is,” he said, gesturing with the gun toward Ammie. “Amelia bears a striking resemblance to her mother.”

Ethan frowned. “Then you did meet Christine on the train?”

"No. As a matter of fact I took great pains to avoid running into her since we'd already taken a lengthy voyage together."

"Voyage?" What voyage? Ethan shook his head to clear away the last of the lingering cobwebs.

"It makes no difference. I'm assuming you are the gentleman who stole Mr. Burgess' dance with Amelia away from him?" When Ethan remain silent, he went on. "And the same one who was on this very beach with her last night?"

"And you're Simeon Hawkes."

The man chuckled. "How gratifying that Lillian and Charles have obviously mentioned me. It's always good to be remembered."

Ethan squinted against the darkness and looked around. "Where's your ghost killer?"

"Is that what you've been calling Mr. Carp?" Hawkes sounded amused by the idea. "Most appropriate, I suppose, if not a bit fanciful." He let out a dramatic sigh. "Unfortunately, his skills diminished with age and he was no longer useful to me."

"Useful like Burgess?"

"Who also met the same fate, although only recently." Hawkes smiled. "His obsession with your ladybird friend was most inconvenient for my plans."

"She's my wife," Ethan growled. "And if you touch her, I'll kill you."

The man laughed but his gun didn't waver. "Your wife? Strange that Mr. Burgess never mentioned that Amelia had a husband. Well, then. I now have a better understanding of your entertaining threat, no matter how gallantly ridiculous it is."

When Ammie suddenly moaned, Ethan tightened his hold on her. "What did they do to Ammie?"

"Nothing to be alarmed at. A little chloroform on a bit of cotton cloth. She'll come around soon." He shrugged. "Hopefully."

Ethan's mind raced as he tried to figure out how to get the gun away from Hawkes without him shooting blindly into the wagon. If he'd been alone, he would have taken that chance. But he couldn't when Ammie was with him.

When Hawkes reached out a hand to poke the tip of Ammie's shoe, Ethan's leg lashed out at him.

"Don't touch her."

Hawkes jumped back to avoid being kicked. "Or what, Amelia's husband? You'll kill me? How do you intend to do that when I'm the one with the gun?" He made a clucking noise with his tongue. "If you're worried I intend to ravish her, set your mind at ease. She isn't to my taste. My plans are a bit more practical, I'm afraid. I want her for the ransom she'll bring."

"Ransom?" Suddenly it became clear to Ethan. Ammie had been Hawkes target all along. To get money from her uncle.

"As I said. I had the pleasure of being on a rather long voyage with Christine Jamison. We spent a good amount of time conversing. When she wasn't boring me with her need to improve her wardrobe, she mentioned how much her brother-in-law loved his niece. I'm sure he'll pay handsomely for her. And it will soothe my offended feelings at having his minions dogging my every step for the last twenty years, among other things."

When Ethan remained silent, a sneer crept into Hawkes' voice. "Come now. Surely he must have mentioned that he owes me for any number of transgressions, even if they did happen before you were even out of the schoolroom."

Ethan shrugged. "For Lillian preferring him over you?"

Hawkes' eyes glittered in the dark. "She chose poorly."

"Then it's revenge you're after?" Ethan's mind raced with desperation. He had to get Hawkes away from Ammie.

"Most assuredly. And the money of course." Hawkes waved his gun. "Get out of the wagon."

When Ethan started to move with Ammie still in his arms, Hawkes shook his head. "No, no. Leave your wife where she is. I need her, but I don't need you."

When Ethan went perfectly still, Hawkes smiled. "Which part of her should I shoot to gain your cooperation? I only need her alive. It doesn't matter if she's crippled or not."

When there was the distinct sound of a gun being cocked, Ethan bent over his wife, trying to protect as much of her as he could. The shot rang out as a bullet slammed into the wagon bed, barely an inch away from Ammie's foot.

Hawkes laughed as he backed up several steps. "Now then. Say your goodbyes and get out of the wagon."

Ethan's heart was pounding in his throat at how close that bullet had come to hitting Ammie. He bent his head and set his lips close to her ear.

"If we only have one day, sweetheart, it was worth it." Trailing his lips slowly along her cheek, he paused to place a soft kiss on her lips. "I love you, Ammie." He set his forehead against hers. "Live, sweetheart. No matter what happens, I'll always be with you. Please live."

Taking in one last breath of her scent, he carefully laid her down and scooted to the edge of the wagon bed.

"Put your hands into the air, and jump down."

Ethan did as he was told, keeping his hands high as he moved away from the wagon, wanting to keep the gun pointing at him and not at Ammie.

"That's far enough."

Hawkes cocked the gun just as Ammie's groggy voice drifted out into the air.

"Ethan?"

Her husband closed his eyes, in his mind seeing her turquoise gaze smiling at him. Just as he always had in his dreams.

The double report of a gun, was followed by a second shot that whizzed past Ethan's cheek and was mingled with Ammie's scream.

Ethan waited for the pain, but nothing came. His eyes flew open and immediately went to Hawkes lying on the ground, blood pouring from one hole in his chest and another in his gut. Just beyond him, Ammie was scrambling over the end of the wagon.

When her legs collapsed, Ethan leaped right over the sprawled-out body between them and grabbed onto her. She threw her arms around his neck and buried her face into his shoulder, sobbing uncontrollably.

As Ethan held his wife close, Charles and Luke stepped out of the shadows, both of them holding rifles still aimed at Hawkes. The gambler lowered his and strode over to the lifeless man, prodding against his side with the toe of his boot.

"Dead," he called out to Luke before turning to face the couple twined together. "Take your wife home, Ethan."

25

Ammie stretched her arms over her head and scooted up to sit higher against the mound of pillows Ethan had stuffed behind her back. Despite everything that had happened the night before, she had never been so rested and happy.

Knowing that nothing from her past would ever again threaten the people she loved today, was enough to put a big smile on her face. And if she never saw her mother again, or never met her grandparents, well, she could live with that. As long as she had Ethan and everyone else in her large extended family, her life was more than perfect.

The door to her bedchamber popped open and Ethan strolled in, carrying a tray in his hands. He grinned at her as he marched across the room and set it down on a table next to the bed.

"I brought you some breakfast."

"I can see that." Ammie eyed the high mound of food on the plates before she burst out laughing. Trust Ethan to make sure she was too stuffed to move.

He leaned over and kissed her, pulling back just far

enough he could look into her eyes. "I want you to keep up your strength, Mrs. Mayes." He wiggled his eyebrows up and down. "I have big plans for us this evening."

Ammie looped her arms around his neck. "As it happens, Mr. Mayes, so do I."

She leaned in and kissed him until he groaned and took a quick step back. "Unless you want those plans to start right now, you'd better behave yourself."

Breaking off a piece of biscuit, Ammie lifted one eyebrow and smiled. "I am behaving."

Ethan laughed and ran a finger down her cheek. "No, you're not. But I'm not complaining." He pointed at the tray. "Now eat something."

She held up her piece of biscuit and waved it back and forth while he shook his head at her. "All right. I promise to eat if you tell me everything that happened last night." She sighed. "I can't remember most of it."

He sat on the edge of the bed and took one of her hands in his. "I'd rather you forgot the whole thing."

"I can't, Ethan," Ammie said softly. "All I remember is seeing Hawkes pointing a gun at you. I was sure he was going to kill you."

"He was sure of it too." When she frowned at him, Ethan gave her a lopsided smile. "Lucky for us that Charles and Luke came along in time to stop him."

Puzzled, Ammie's brow furrowed as she tried to reason it out. "I don't understand how they found us so quickly."

"No mystery there, sweetheart. Your uncle has had us followed since the day Christine showed up with her warning about Hawkes." Ethan sighed as he shook his head. "Lillian came by this morning, and told me that Charles had been sure Hawkes would try to get to him. Either through an ambush, or someone he loved. And that not only included his wife and children, but you and Charlotte too."

He cradled her face in his hands and kissed her again.

"I'm sorry, Ammie," he said softly. "It never occurred to me he might use you as a weapon against your uncle."

"It never occurred to me either," Ammie admitted. "I was only a child when my father was murdered. I didn't think Hawkes even knew I existed. How did he find out?"

Ethan shrugged. "It doesn't make any difference. He's dead. That's the end of it."

Nodding her agreement, Ammie laced her fingers with his. "I still don't understand how Uncle Charles had us followed without you knowing about it. You spotted me easily enough from across the square."

Ethan laughed. "I'd spot you, sweetheart, if you were on the other side of the world." When she rolled her eyes, he grinned. "I probably would have seen someone tailing us if your uncle had used his usual guards, but he had Master Kwan hire them."

"Master Kwan?" Ammie's eyes opened wide in astonishment. "Is that where Wang Wei has been all this time? Following us?"

"He has. When he realized what was happening, he tied a bag of colored rock dust that Henry had given him to the bottom of the wagon. It leaked out while Wang Wei ran to warn Charles." Ethan's eyes glowed with amusement. "By the time the rock dust in the bag ran out, Charles and Luke had a good idea where the wagon was headed, and since they moved a lot faster than that old wagon, they weren't far behind us."

Ammie leaned over until her mouth was just a breath away from his. "I'm so glad that Henry is so fascinated with rocks."

TWO DAYS LATER, Ammie walked down the stairs with Dorrie. The two women had spent a good hour going over plans for the wedding celebration Aunt Charlotte was insisting on giving for the entire family. It would take several weeks to get them all into town, but her aunt was determined to do it.

Lillian was standing in the foyer, her cloak in place and her reticule in her hand when she looked up and smiled at the two younger women. "Are you ready to go to Maggie's? She's impatient to hear all about what happened, and intends to get the entire story while you're being fitted for your gown, Ammie."

Dorrie slipped an arm around her friend's waist. "Mam told me not to step one foot into her shop unless you were with me."

Ammie laughed. "She told Aunt Charlotte she wouldn't start one stitch on my dress until she heard every detail about what happened with Hawkes."

"Then we'd best be on our way. I understand she's bought yards of lace for your dress, and we don't want it to go to waste." Lillian ushered them out the door toward the waiting carriage.

The next several hours passed in a pleasant flurry of satin, lace, and a cozy gossip. Maggie was properly horrified over what Hawkes had tried to do, and Ammie was thoroughly enchanted with the dress the seamstress was making for her.

Once they'd been shooed out of the shop so Maggie could get some serious work done, the three women stood on the sidewalk as Dorrie put two hands against the small of her back. "I'd love to have a cup of tea at Kate's, but wish I didn't have to get back into that carriage yet."

Lillian gave her a sympathetic smile. "If you're feeling up to it, we could walk there. Her shop is just on the other side of the square."

Dorrie nodded eagerly. "I think that's a wonderful idea." She glanced over at Ammie. "Do you mind if we walk?"

Sure she'd enjoy stretching her legs after sitting so long while Maggie had brought out dozens of cloth samples for her to look at, Ammie smiled at the expectant mother. "I think it's a wonderful idea."

Lillian turned to tell the carriage driver to meet them to Kate's as Ammie slipped an arm through Dorrie's and started down the street.

"You know, I doubt if my husband will ever set foot in Kate's again." Ammie leaned closer to Dorrie's ear. "He says the chairs aren't sturdy enough."

"So does Jules," Dorrie laughed.

Lillian came up beside them just in time to hear their exchange. "I stopped taking Charles there long ago. Whenever we left Kate's, we had to go directly to The Crimson Rose so Cook could fix him something worth eating." She shook her head. "It was annoying."

The three women were still laughing when they started to cross the square toward the tea shop. Halfway to the other side, Ammie stopped dead in her tracks.

Ethan stood in the center of the path, dressed in the same formal clothes he'd worn the first time they'd danced together. Catching and holding her gaze, he walked slowly toward Ammie, holding out a crimson rose.

~

Ethan smiled when Ammie's eyes grew as big as the saucers she placed her teacups on. His whole body tightened when her lips trembled into a smile and a sheen of moisture appeared in her eyes. He'd never get used to how beautiful she was, or how much he loved her.

He blocked out everything but the two of them and kept walking until he was within a foot of her. Breaking off the head of the rose, he carefully placed the vivid bloom in her hair. When she reached up to touch it, he captured her hand and held it against his lips as he sank down on one knee.

"Amelia Jamison, you are the love of my life, and you always have been. I can't even breathe without you, because when your aren't with me, I have no life at all." Ethan reached into his pocket. When his hand reappeared it was holding a ring, the diamond in its center flashing fire in the afternoon light. He held it up to her.

"Marry me."

Ammie laid her free hand along the side of his face and gifted him with the most magical smile he'd ever seen.

"Yes."

He rose and slipped the ring onto her finger while several voices around them called out, "kiss her".

Thinking it was an excellent idea, Ethan wrapped his arms around the woman he'd loved ever since he was twelve years old, and lowered his head to hers.

As their lips met, tears streamed down Dorrie's and Lillian's faces, while the entire square erupted into applause.

But neither Ethan nor Ammie heard them as they happily drifted in a world of their own.

26

Ethan stood between Jules and Robbie, watching with an amused grin as the women of the family scurried in and out of the very elegant parlor in Lillian and Charles' home, readying everything for the wedding celebration that would be taking place that night. It had indeed taken Charlotte almost a month to get the whole family rounded up and in town at the same time, but the determined Southern belle had managed it, and was now looking very pleased with herself as she arranged pink flowers in a tall vase and chatted with Lillian.

At the other end of the room, Dorrie and Brenna were in a serious discussion over the placement of some chairs, while Ammie looked on, her foot tapping a rapid beat against the thick rug at her fee. When his bride glanced over at her husband and made a face, Ethan raised the whiskey glass in his hand as a salute to her efforts and winked back at her, making her laugh.

As he smiled at the sound, Robbie gave him a poke in the side with his elbow. "Keep showing that stupid-looking grin and I'm going to start to think you like being married."

Not bothering with more than a shrug, Ethan's eyes followed his wife as she moved about the room. He was looking forward to seeing Ammie in the lace and satin gown Maggie had fashioned for her, and even more to taking it off of her later on that evening.

"You know the women in the family don't consider you properly married until there's an acceptable proposal and a big party," Jules laughed. "There hasn't been a party yet, so you could still get out of this whole thing, grab some stock from the stable here in town, and head on north."

"Not a chance in hell," Ethan immediately responded.

"I'm afraid he's hogtied for good after getting down on one knee in the middle of the square." Robbie imitated Ethan's earlier gesture and raised his own whiskey glass at his friend. "Makes the rest of us look bad. Of course, that's the only way he'd ever be forgiven for dragging Ammie to a preacher who goes by the name of 'Rabbit'."

"Never thought I'd see the day Ethan Mayes would make such a fool of himself in public over a woman," Jules agreed. "Wish I could have seen it."

"Glad you didn't," Ethan grumbled. He was fairly certain he wasn't going to hear the end of it as it was, much less if his two friends had been there to witness it. But he still had no regrets. The sheer happiness reflected on Ammie's face would stay with him forever.

Robbie clapped a hand on Ethan's shoulder. "Some women are worth it. Brenna sure is."

Jules nodded his agreement. "So is Dorrie."

"We all got lucky," Ethan said quietly.

He didn't know how it had happened, but by a pure miracle, Ammie loved him back. Something he'd never even let himself dream of had come true despite all of his efforts to run away from it. And it had become all that more perfect when Luke had given his stables to Ethan as a wedding present.

Last week Ammie had helped him moved into town permanently, and they'd spent several enjoyable hours since then looking for a house of their own—at Aunt Charlotte's insistence.

Ethan was glad he'd still be working with the animals during the day, and helping Ammie with her Inquiries business in the evening. Purely to be sure she didn't get into any trouble. And at night, he'd be holding her in his arms until the sun rose again.

Whenever he really took the time to consider it, Ethan knew he was the luckiest man alive. He raised his glass again and grinned at the two men standing next to him.

"May we always be grateful for the good women who love us."

"I can't argue with that." Jules took a long sip then raised an eyebrow at Robbie who'd taken a quick drink before placing his glass on the nearest table.

"All this talk about our wives has put me in the mood to show mine a bit of gratitude right now." The tall rancher strolled off to the sound of deep laughter behind him.

"That's not a bad idea," Jules said, setting his own glass aside. "Think I'll see if I can sweet talk Dorrie into sitting down for a spell."

Ethan took one last sip of his drink before putting his glass next to the other two and crossing the room until he was standing right behind Ammie. He leaned down to whisper into her ear.

"There isn't a man in this room who loves his wife more than I do mine."

Ammie turned around and looped her arms around his neck, her eyes shining as she gazed up at him. “Oh really?”

“Yes, Mrs. Mayes, really.”

He grinned and lowered his head and proceeded to thoroughly kiss his Ammie, exactly the way he meant to do for the rest of their lives.

AUTHOR'S NOTE

To My Readers ~

I hope you enjoyed Ethan and Ammie's story. I've waited quite a while to finally bring to justice the man who had Ammie's father murdered—and was happy when it was Cracker, the young thief from Only One Promise, who ended up being the perfect man for Ammie. I loved writing about Ethan and Amelia—two people who are so sure they aren't good enough for each other, and never afraid to face new adventures. These two deserved to be together at last.

I want to take this opportunity to thank you, the reader. Time is precious, and I so appreciate you spending some of yours to read my books. I enjoy writing, and am very lucky to be able to do just that. And even luckier to have someone read my stories.

Thank you, and happy reading!

Cathryn Chandler

You can pick-up the any of my other romance novels on Amazon, or read for free with your Kindle Unlimited membership!

Be the first to receive notification of the release of the next novel in my romance series. **Sign up** today at:

http://eepurl.com/bLBOtX

If you'd like to know what my latest projects are, and how they're coming along, drop by my website at:

www.CathrynChandler.com

Follow Cathryn Chandler on your favorite media:

Facebook:

https://www.facebook.com/cathrynchandlerauthor/?fref=ts

Twitter: @catcauthor

Website/blog: www.cathrynchandler.com

All authors strive to deliver the highest quality work to their readers. If you found a spelling or typographical error in this book, please let me know so I can correct it immediately. Please use the contact form on my website at: www.cathrynchandler.com Thank you!

And finally: If you like mysteries, I also write those under the pen name: Cat Chandler, and they are also available on Amazon.

Made in the USA
Monee, IL
20 January 2022